THE HANDLER

THE HANDLER

THE YACHT CLUB SERIES

JORDYN KROSS

Scarlet Parlor Press, LLC

Published by Scarlet Parlor Press, LLC

Editor: Jenny Sims

Cover: Brandi Doane McCann

Library of Congress Control Number: 2023921594

Names: Kross, Jordyn, author.
Title: The handler / Jordyn Kross.
Description: [Albuquerque, New Mexico] : Scarlet Parlor Press, LLC, [2023] | Series: The yacht club series
Identifiers: ISBN: 978-1-959691-03-7 (paperback) | 978-1-959691-02-0 (ebook)
Subjects: LCSH: Intelligence officers--United States--Fiction. | United States. Federal Bureau of Investigation--Fiction. | Man-woman relationships--Fiction. | Witnesses--Protection--Fiction. | Gangsters--Fiction. | Impersonation--Fiction. | Danger--Fiction. | LCGFT: Erotic fiction. | Romance fiction. | Thrillers (Fiction) | BISAC: FICTION / Romance / Erotic. | FICTION / Romance / Contemporary. | FICTION / Romance / Suspense.
Classification: LCC: PS3611.R776 H36 2023 | DDC: 813/.6--dc23

ALSO BY JORDYN KROSS

Find all of Jordyn's books at jordynkross.com or here:

Melting Hearts Series

Prequel Novella - Jack's Frost

(free for newsletter subscribers)

Book 1 - Winter's List

Book 2 - Xmas Angel

Book 3 - Shattered Ice

Dirty Daisy Mystery Series

Book 1 - Dirty Daisy

Book 2 - Hell Hath No Furry

Uhraervi Brothers

Open Enrollment

Hung with Care

Pole Position

NOAH Series

Prequel Novella - Quantum Entanglements

Nonfiction

Demystifying the Beats

Single Titles

A Lost Claus

For "the ladies," who always support me and whose friendship means the world to me.

ONE

Amy

"AMY?"

I look up when the new president of the Alabaster Bed-and-Breakfast Association calls my name. Except I'm not Amy. Amy is the name *he* gave me when I agreed to testify in a racketeering case three years ago. Three long years. I never expected to be in hiding in a tiny Colorado mountain town this long. Whatever fire I had in my belly to see justice done has cooled in the past few months. Now I just want to live a normal life, have friends, participate in the community, and meet a man who could love me—be my life partner—make a family with me. If he likes to spank my ass occasionally, that's even better.

I twist the plain gold band on my left hand. I was alone even before I moved to Colorado. Now, being alone feels lonely. An unfamiliar heaviness has settled in my heart. My dream of running an inn is vastly different from the reality. The long days on my own rush by in a blur of years. I used to have all the time in the world, or I thought I did. I haven't had an adventure or done something new, something just for myself, since the day I got brave enough to join the club in St. Louis. My heart races like it did the first time I opened that dungeon door. Like it did the first time I saw him. The first time I let him—

"Amy, dear? Are you okay? You're flushed."

I rush back to the present in a flood of regret. Deborah Budnek is a sweet lady who's run an inn for twenty years. I can only imagine her expression if I answer honestly. Instead, I smile. "Too much coffee this morning. Are we ready for the meeting? Need me to do anything?"

"We're all set, as long as you have the treasurer's report."

"Right here." I pat my laptop bag. Deborah's jaw would hit the floor if she knew I used to be a certified accountant. She thinks I'm an innkeeper with basic bookkeeping skills. According to my witness security agreement, I'm not supposed to do anything with numbers. But what my handler doesn't know won't hurt him. It's just a teeny-tiny not-for-profit I'm volunteering to help. Not like I offered to start doing the members' taxes.

I move behind the oblong folding table set up for us in the community room of the Aspen library. Alabaster's library is as small as the town and doesn't have room. Not that I mind the large windows and modern space, but the traffic in this elite tourist town is a nightmare, no matter the season. It's the reason I use to explain why I rarely make the drive if anyone asks. The truth is, if anyone ever recognized me—

"Am I late?" Katherine, my New York heiress friend, dashes in, looking like a million dollars in jeans and a silk top with her blond hair in its signature twist. I'm pretty sure her outfit was custom-made for her, unlike my jeans and boatneck top from the outlet stores in Castlerock. But I'm supposed to blend in, something Katherine could never do—even if she wore cheap outlet clothes.

Several women and a few men sitting in the folding chairs organized in rows turn and greet the woman who has helped them save their businesses. My friend is a magician with marketing and websites.

Before I can greet her, the secretary and vice president take their seats, and Deborah calls the meeting to order.

"THAT WAS SHORT AND SWEET." Katherine tucks her arm into mine as we walk out into the late summer sunshine. The sky is cobalt blue, and a few white fluffy clouds lounge around with no intention of providing rain.

"Vastly different from when Betty was in charge," I agree. Betty Keppel was a horrible leader, but nowhere near as awful as my last boss. A chill runs up my spine. "I don't miss the shame sessions."

"Lunch?" Katherine asks. "My treat. I have to babble about the wedding plans. And Gabe will back out if I keep harassing him about colors and flowers."

I laugh. Gabe—a former soldier and Katherine's fiancé—is a total sweetheart. "Yeah, he's made it very clear he is not into decorating or making things pretty."

"Fortunately, he has me." Katherine tapped her chest. "And you. The wedding will be perfect."

I'll do everything I can to help make sure Katherine has the fairy-tale experience she deserves. My own wedding wasn't notable. A judge and a piece of paper. I haven't seen my "husband" in almost a year. He usually calls me about every six weeks, but I haven't heard from him in...three months?

The afternoon sun glints off my gold band, heavy on my finger. The void of longing that I keep carefully closed off gapes open for a brief second, spiking pain through my chest.

Maybe he's forgotten me.

If only I could do the same.

TWO

Tyler

I SET my coffee on the coaster and settle into my ergonomic black mesh chair. With a flick of the switch, my computer comes to life. Thank god maintenance fixed the air-conditioning. Summer in Missouri is a killer. I'm definitely going to grab lunch in the cafeteria so I don't have to go back out. The St. Louis FBI field office might look like a concrete and mirrored-glass bunker out of the sixties, but it has its perks.

I double verify my identity and dig into my latest security briefings. Occasionally, there's a nugget, a detail I haven't considered in my templates for a mass casualty response. Humans are damn creative, and every time a security hole is closed, they dig a little deeper and find the next tiny crack in the facade to exploit. Today, each file reassures me that my plans are tight. While nothing is ever completely quiet, I might be able to make it through the weekend without a significant event.

After twenty-five years, first as an investigative specialist, then a victim specialist, and most recently as a mass casualty response team coordinator, quiet routine is a welcome friend. Done with the briefings, I check the analog clock on the wall. Not quite time for lunch. I could take care of some office tasks or chat with a co-worker, saving the rest of my email until the afternoon. Before deciding, I scan the list of senders. One name pops—John Clemmons, a friend and a federal marshal.

Hey Tyler,

Heads-up. Enzo Brambilla bought the farm. Not going to be a trial. Your special guest will be removed from the program at the end of the month. Nothing I could do. Budgets.

I'm supposed to send her an email to close out the file. You want me to hold off? Let you handle it?

Need to know ASAP.

JC

No fucking way. Enzo is mob. His death doesn't remove the blade hanging over Amy's head. I shoot off a quick reply, thanking John and taking responsibility for the notification. Sending me an email about the witness isn't completely kosher, but like I give a shit. I minimize my email and open File Explorer.

Deep in my computer files hides the single most important one—encrypted and password protected. One I shouldn't have. One I've been trying to ignore, to let some space cool my attraction. The folder opens, and I click on her picture. Her face fills my screen—soft brown hair curls over her shoulders. Sweet brown eyes meet mine. Lips posed in a delicate pout, begging me to kiss them. Well, not really. Not at all. That's just the story I've told myself over the past few years. No matter how long I avoid contact, I'll never get over her.

I was still in victims' assistance when I took her case. She had racketeering evidence against a mobster who'd been on the radar for a long time. I should have recused myself from her investigation since we had prior contact before she called in the report. But we agreed, and neither of us said a thing.

So she's mine.

If the agency knew how true that was, I'd be fired on the spot. I've been living on borrowed time, holding this secret, counting on the trial finishing before my security clearance came up for renewal. My one tainted action in an exemplary record. I push back my chair, ignoring the smack of it hitting the window, and march to my boss's office.

"Tyler, just who I need to see." Special Agent in Charge McCarty gestures to one of the chairs across from his desk.

I drop into it and will my leg to stop bouncing. I can't reveal how agitated I am.

"Just hung up with the attorney general's office. One of our perps died last night in prison. Enzo Brambilla Sr. Natural causes. The case has been dropped. No perp, no trial. Think that was the last one of your field cases."

I keep my face blank as if I don't already know, as if I'm not dying to get to my girl to protect her. "There's the matter of the witness. My victim."

"Not anymore. The case is closed. Neither of you will have to testify. Marshals will take care of whatever needs to be done on the witness end."

The words punch me in the gut. No protection. "The guy's a mob boss. Just because Senior's dead doesn't mean the family won't still go after her."

"Budgets." McCarty shrugs. "Besides, the Brambilla family has been moving toward more and more legal enterprises."

Bullshit. I swallow the scream and keep my face neutral. "Can I request a formal review?"

"You can. But these days, the money's all tied up in preventing domestic terrorism. A simple racketeering case doesn't have the same level of visibility. These aren't the J. Edgar days."

"Right. Anything else?" I have to get out of here before I say or do something stupid.

"Close out the file."

I clamp my jaw shut and leave. Back in my office, I spin in my chair and stare out the large rectangular window at the perfectly manicured lawn and the black metal fence beyond.

Close the file?

How am I supposed to turn my back on the woman I've protected for years?

If I push the review, it'll burn a bridge with SAC McCarty. And he's right—the committee will most likely turn me down. But I have to do something. After submitting a vacation request, I stare at my email inbox, desperate for an answer.

"HE FUCKING DENIED MY VACATION." I smack the edge of the bar and stare at Master Stone. The gray taking over his dark hair and the sun-aged skin puts him at maybe a decade older than me. It's hard to tell because he keeps himself at the military-level fitness of a thirty-year-old. He's a mentor to me at the club, to all the Dominants, and has talked me down from a bad decision more than once.

"How long have you been in?" His voice is gravel under the wheels of a Harley.

"The FBI?"

"Long enough to retire?"

The question smacks me between the eyes like a baseball bat. Retire? I've never thought about it. Never wanted to work somewhere else. I'm eligible for my pension. And I've had additional deductions taken from my paycheck to lower my taxes, but I don't even track the accumulated balance, especially after the last couple of market crashes. I leave that to my accountant. But there are other assets too, mostly the result of having had a financial planner for a mother. I assumed I would die on the job well before I ever got to retirement.

Stone nudges me with his shoulder. "Doesn't mean you have to stop working. But you could deal with your woman, then figure out what to do next."

Past the rectangular bar set in the middle of the floor, the stage features a Dom I don't know using a crop on a sub restrained to a padded bench. The usual urge I have to find a willing sub is missing. Over the past few years, I've lost any motivation to participate in meaningless scenes. Only one woman should feel the impact of my present frustration, but she's in Colorado. Stone guides us to a booth, and I slide in.

The last time Amelia Kincaid, now Davis, and I shared a scene, I almost convinced her to come home with me.

If I'd known it would be our last time together at the club, I might have pushed harder. But then I wouldn't have been able to skirt the rule about being involved with her case. As it is, I stretched the rules way too far to pass scrutiny.

Four other Doms saunter over to our booth. Alex shuffles in next to me. In his slow Texas drawl, he asks, "What's up, Master T? You look like you got kicked by a mule."

I hesitate for a second. Alex may be young, but he's an old soul and someone I count as a trusted friend. "You remember Mia?"

He nods and takes a pull off his bottle of beer.

"She's in danger."

Seated between his business partners, Cade and Eliot, Blake puts his forearms on the table, and his sun-bleached hair flops forward. "I thought she moved away years ago. How could you know she's at risk?"

"I've kept tabs." I can't say more without disclosing all the rules I've broken. Stone likely suspects, but the man is a vault.

Eliot stretches his six-foot frame back in the chair he'd pulled up to the booth. He eyes me, calculating. His curly hair is clipped close to his head in a fade, his nails perfectly mani-cured, and his black shirt tucked neatly into dark denim. A shadow except for those piercing hazel eyes that are surgically taking me apart.

"Theoretically, I don't know where she is." Though she's technically no longer in WITSEC, I still hesitate to speak about her location in public.

Eliot crosses his arms, his gaze still locked on me. "Theory." He snorts. "Go to where you don't know she is and bring her home. That's what we'd do."

Blake and Cade nod.

Bringing my sweet sub back to St. Louis would put her closer to the Brambilla family, so that doesn't seem like a good idea. It would only make the bad guys' job easier because, unlike my boss, I know the mob still has a hard-on for her. And if I go out there, knowing she's no longer under federal marshal protection, it would be impossible to leave.

"She's not in Missouri," I admit.

"Figured as much." Eliot shrugs.

"Whatever you decide," Stone says, "we have your back. If you need us—"

"We're there, dude." Alex smacks his bottle on the table like a judge's gavel.

Slowly, Eliot moves forward, putting his elbow on the table and resting his chin on his fist. "We can provide security." His deep voice rolls across the table like fog. "The three of us. Reed's on an extended bodyguard contract."

I swallow down the gooey feelings choking me at all this loyalty. Knowing I have backup makes my decision easier. I'll call her on Monday and set some guidelines to hold her over until I can explain in person.

IN MY OFFICE, I make an X on the calendar that hangs on my wall.

"Counting the days, I see." McCarty leans on my doorjamb with his thermal coffee cup clutched in his hand. He's been a good boss, but the urge to deck him has me tapping my red marker against the desk. "I came by to ask if you're sure about retiring. Hard to replace agents as cool-headed and dedicated as you." He shrugs. "Guess there's no changing your mind?"

He should have reminded himself how valuable I was to the agency when he denied my vacation request. I force an easy smile. "Nope."

Only five more days to go. A plane ticket sits in my personal email. My checked luggage is already packed, so I only have to fill my carry-on. The rental car will be waiting at the Denver airport. One more week and I'll be able to see her in person for the first time in...almost a year. I can't believe I haven't been to Alabaster in over ten months. Not since I last had a vacation request approved. It's well past time to retire, even if taking care of this issue with Amy is temporary.

I'll go out there and set her up with more security and maybe another new identity. New location. I have no reason to believe she wants me. Despite watching over her for years, she's hasn't reciprocated my attraction. Once she's safe and secure, I can figure out what I want to do next. Maybe I'll take up fishing or golf or model trains like a million other old guys. Except at forty-seven, I don't feel old yet, and I've only ever been an agent.

The empty doorway to a sterile hallway captures everything wrong with my life. After I leave here, no one will wait to see if I come in. Fuck. I shake off this existential hangover and log into my computer.

A red banner with an alert triangle in the header smacks me in the face, and dread ties my stomach in knots. I click it, expecting to be on a plane coordinating a team in the next hour. Who knows how many days I'll be on-site dealing with the latest disaster.

Alert. Document filed with Internal Revenue Service.

IRS? What the...?

It's not a mass casualty event. It's not even an event. It's a 990-N filing for a not-for-profit in Colorado. The treasurer's name and the filing location of Alabaster triggered my custom rule, Amy Davis. The name I gave her when the marshals placed her into the witness security program. I shouldn't have been involved. No one outside the handler was supposed to know her secret identity and location, but I know all her secrets. As I explained when she entered the program, "John is your handler on paper, but *I'm* your handler in reality."

I drill down into what caused the alert. Within minutes, I have my answer and a rage headache. Amy Davis is a principal officer of a not-for-profit organization incorporated in Colorado. She's listed as the treasurer. The fucking treasurer. The postcard-sized document that triggered the warning bears her signature. Is she trying to get killed?

My hidden encrypted file has her cell number. I can't risk keeping it in my contacts. Opening it, I bring up the picture of her face again. Too bad the profile doesn't include the image of her heart-shaped ass, which was made for spanking. Luckily, the memory has never faded. I'll refresh it as soon as I can get to her and ask what the hell she thinks she's doing.

Her phone rings through to voicemail. "Call me."

I hang up, close the picture, and grip the desk, fighting the urge to say fuck it all and get on a plane today.

THREE

Amy

THE FLOWERS from the hotel garden will have to do. Poor Katherine. She spent so much time planning the perfect outdoor wedding to Gabe, and everything that could go wrong is going *terribly* wrong. From the torrential rain to the frozen flower arrangements—what's next?

At least I'm here for my friend. And the satin sheath dress she picked for me is gorgeous with its gauzy watercolor roses overlay. My heels sink into the ornately patterned runner that flows down the wood plank hallways. The venue is a beautiful historic hotel with widely spaced doors marked with brass numbers. I'm enchanted by the local artists' works used to break up the pale mint walls. In a place like this and marrying a man like Gabe, Katherine should have a perfect fairy-tale wedding.

I could have told her those happily-ever-after stories were fiction, but why bother ruining the day before it happens?

Especially when Mother Nature seems to have things well in hand in the "ruining things" department.

As I head toward Katherine's dressing room, I fuss with the thick twine holding the autumn cuttings together—a couple of sunflowers, mums, asters, some rosemary, and everything else I could make work. I'm good at making things work and fixing problems as they arise. I wish someone could have made everything okay when my own life fell apart three years ago. Tyler kind of provided that, except he isn't a friend. He's...complicated. And he's been calling way too much since Papa Enzo died and I was removed from WITSEC. I don't have time to deal with that, not right now. One more day and I'll—

No.

I freeze.

My heart rises to my throat.

Tyler stands right outside Katherine's door. His glower travels the length of the hallway and grips the back of my neck. Fuck. He's pissed off—at me. Despite his rumpled suit, he still looks like the sexy, powerful Dom who captivated me years ago. His crossed muscular arms help the vibe. I move a few feet closer, trying to ignore the flutter in my belly. Not a streak of gray mars his golden-brown curls, the same as always—long and curly on top and nearly nonexistent on the sides. His bronze skin still looks like he just spent a week on the beach.

"What are you doing here?" I ask before he gets a chance to take control. His forest-green eyes are on fire.

"You didn't return my calls. That's not what we agreed to. After forty-eight hours with no contact, I followed protocol." Tyler's voice is perfectly Midwest with no accent, but the command in his tone touches me intimately in a way he hasn't achieved over the phone. Something about him in person— pissed off and growly—takes me right back to the club days.

I shake it off. I talked to him three—okay maybe four—days ago. "I've been busy with this wedding. I'm *still* busy."

"And with the treasurer's job for ABBA, too, I assume?"

Crap. He wasn't supposed to know about that. Enzo's dead. "It's a tiny organization. No one's going to notice."

"*I* noticed."

"You're supposed to." At least I guess that's his job since he seems to be good at it. "Leave or take a seat. I have to take care of this bouquet."

"I'll save you a seat."

Why does that sound like a threat to my ass? "I'm the bridesmaid. I mean, matron of honor. I won't be sitting."

"If you don't join me as soon as the ceremony is over, you're damn right you won't be." He slides a lock of my hair through his fingers, giving it a tiny tug, his eyes smoldering.

Guess I was right about that threat to my backside. My pussy quivers, begging for me to agree. "As if. Those days are over."

"Not for me." He steps back, allowing me to enter Katherine's room.

I rush in, clutching the bunch of flowers like a lifeline. Katherine fiddles with her earrings, pretending she hasn't overheard my conversation in the hallway.

"I can't believe him," I say.

"Who?" Katherine widens her eyes, still trying to feign ignorance.

"My hand—husband." Dammit. I nearly slipped.

"He's here, in town?"

Katherine probably thought I lied about having a husband. But no, he's here. In the damn sexy flesh. "Unexpectedly."

"At least you have a date for the reception now."

A date? I blink at her. I haven't had a date...since before everything with Enzo Jr. In fact, Tyler and I never dated before

I signed that marriage certificate. Never even kissed, before or after. I can't deal with this now. I hold up the bouquet. "An original arrangement, courtesy of the hotel garden."

"It's beautiful. Thank you." Katherine takes the late-season arrangement. "You're a lifesaver."

A few minutes later, her estranged father knocks on the door, asking to walk her down the aisle. Stepping aside, I let him in. I have no idea if Katherine will let him escort her, but I wish I still had family—even an asshole. I don't have anyone to be mad at.

Tears choke in my throat.

I have to get out of this room. I latch on to the sound of the piano, indicating it's time for the ceremony to start.

"Meet you out there," I tell Katherine before I escape.

Tyler comes to attention as soon as I step out.

"Why are you still here?" I hiss at him. Is it too much to ask for a few minutes alone to process all this heartache before I have to stand in front of all the wedding guests with a smile on my face?

"You'll open the door to anyone. Do you have any sense of self-preservation?"

If I did, I'd be avoiding him. Instead, I let him take my hand and lead me to the garden doors. He sits at the back of the small gathering of chairs the staff has just finished wiping down. Hopefully, that's the last of the waterworks.

IT WILL BE a miracle if I make it through this event without tears. The ceremony drew every emotion out of me. Katherine and Gabe's love is the kind every girl dreams of finding. The rain paused long enough for them to exchange their vows. Heartfelt, soul-deep words of commitment. Words I'll never hear. Because I'm already married to the man next to me, who might as well be a stranger, despite the intimate *sessions* we've shared in the past. Heat creeps up my cheeks.

Tyler pulls out my chair. I introduce him to Sebastian, the young man Katherine and Gabe—and to the extent I could—cared for through his high school years, and his mother. Sebastian did an admirable job as Gabe's best man.

"Who's this?" Sebastian's mom asks Tyler in a flirty tone.

He tells her he's my husband, and I have to resist the urge to slug him. Not because he's lying but because it's such a farce after what we witnessed earlier out on the rain-soaked lawn. The servers place our plates, and thankfully, the topic changes to the food. I glance over at the Sweetheart table. Katherine and Gabe are eating their delicious dinner, glowing with happiness. I can't taste a thing.

Tyler leans over and whispers, "I always saw you as a spring bride."

I narrow my eyes and lean in close like we're sharing a loving conversation. "As if we would ever have a wedding. I signed a piece of paper in front of a judge. Are we even married since my legal name is not even on the certificate?"

"Papers were filed, *Amy*." His emphasis on my name—the name he chose—only adds to my distress.

It all came down to papers when he made me disappear for my own good. A new name, a shiny new marriage, a new home, a new job, a new life where I have to do everything exactly right or risk the wrath of a mob family. Even my taxes are designated as married filing separately. What a sad status. Being disconnected from the person I should be closest to. I finally ask the one question that has weighed on me since that whirlwind day when I became a new woman with a new husband: "Why?"

He mutters something about power of attorney and medical

events before quickly initiating a conversation with Sebastian about his life at college.

Something about his reasoning is bullshit, but this is not the time or the place to figure it out. I smile and try to make polite conversation with Sebastian's birth mom. Despite the horrible way she treated Sebastian, Katherine and I have included her in Sebastian's life. She's really not a terrible person, just a terrible mom. Sebastian is doing surprisingly well, mostly thanks to Katherine and Gabe, but I do what I can. Becoming a foster mom myself would break too many rules.

After dinner, the rain kicks up again, and Katherine and Gabe make the wise decision to skip the dancing and head for the cake. The tent sways with the wind. It's as if Tyler brought the storm with him to reflect his terrible mood. He's done a good job of hiding it, but it simmers under the surface, waiting to be unleashed.

Katherine navigates a sea of platinum damask-covered round tables and well-dressed guests to hand me her last-minute bouquet. "Thank you," she says. "You went to so much trouble to get these flowers for me. You should have them."

"Breaking the tradition of tossing the bouquet?" I tease, avoiding all my wishes and what-ifs as I take the arrangement.

"I think Gabe's sister is the only single woman here, and with her five brothers, that'll be her status for a while."

Katherine and I laugh, and I give her a quick hug. "Have a wonderful time on your honeymoon. Call me for anything."

Katherine squeezes me again before moving around the table. She kisses Sebastian on the cheek and tells him she loves him. "I'll see you at fall break. Amy will be here. I'll keep my cell phone on. And be careful on the drive back to school."

She sounds like a mother despite never having given birth. Another experience I'll never have, thanks to the stupid Brambilla family. At thirty-seven, the window of opportunity for having children is swiftly closing.

"I'll be fine." Sebastian stands and hugs Katherine. "Love you, too."

I swallow down my thread of jealousy. Katherine has a family. Even Gabe's sister, who couldn't receive the bouquet because of her overprotective brothers, is blessed with family. I glance at Tyler. I have a handler.

The hotel staff swarms the tent as soon as Katherine and Gabe leave. Most of the guests are quickly following. I look at Sebastian and ask, "Ready to go?"

"Are you sure it's okay if we stay with you?" his mom asks.

"Of course. It's my pleasure to have you, and the rooms are ready." I prepped the two rooms yesterday during a whirlwind of activity.

"Thank you for having us," she says. She's become much nicer over the years. Maybe she figured out Sebastian needed more than she could give him. Or maybe she's happy someone else stepped up to fill her shoes. I'm too tired to figure it out. As soon as I hit my bed, I'm going to sleep for a day.

Tyler plucks my keys out of my hand. "I'm driving."

"But—"

"You had wine at dinner. You're swaying in your shoes from exhaustion, and it's a thirty-minute drive to the Sunflower."

I hate that he's right. "What about your car? I assume you rented one."

"We can pick it up tomorrow. Just need to grab my bags." He tucks my hand in his elbow, and we race through the rain to my little white four-door sedan.

The trip home lasts a minute. I must have slept on the way. As soon as I get inside, I start the kettle out of habit, but I need the warm comfort of a cup of tea after a rainy, unexpectedly harried day. Thankfully, Sebastian and his mom quickly settle in their rooms, and my other guests seem content as well. No messages to deal with. No guests sitting in the great room. Clutching my half-empty cup, I drag myself up the first two stairs and pause. Tyler is right behind me. I gaze up to the top of the stairs and pray for this day to be a dream because it has officially become a nightmare. "I don't have another room."

Tyler joins me on the same tread, his hand on my lower back. "Lead the way, wife."

The surge of energy that comes with the impulse to stab this infuriating man fuels the remainder of my journey. Too bad it doesn't last long enough to kick him out and tell him to find another place to stay. Plus, I can't send him back out into this weather. Lightning flashes, illuminating the dark room. Is it a sign that I'm making a big mistake?

"This is my side." I point at the bed. "Bathroom's through there. I'm first." With my most conservative pair of flannel pajamas in hand, I duck into the small room with the tiny shower and try to figure out how my life became such a mess.

A knock on the door motivates me to finish brushing my teeth. I duck around Tyler as I exit, brushing against his hard body. I'm sure he notices my shiver. "All yours."

When Tyler quickly reappears in nothing but gray sweatpants, I consider stealing his pillow to cover my eyes. His tanned abs are carved into a six-pack. The slight V of his Adonis belt peeks above his waistband. And based on the bulge at the top of his thighs, he's got plenty to work with in the sex department. The man is too attractive, and my imagination is a traitorous slut.

"Why are you here?" My nasty tone is designed to kill any urges he—or really I—might be having.

He ducks, the slant of the roof making it impossible to stand upright as he slides into the other side of *my* bed.

"Despite Enzo Senior's death and the trial not moving forward, I don't believe you're out of danger. I tried to convince everyone to keep you in the program, but..." He shrugs one shoulder. "I'm not going to leave you unprotected." His gaze locks onto me, and he tucks a tendril of my hair back. "You're mine."

The cool room is suddenly stifling. I shift away from him, right to the edge of the bed. "I'm not."

He rolls back, hands under his head, staring at the ceiling. "My case. My responsibility."

His clarification doesn't make it any more palatable. I'm not anyone's but mine. "What are you going to do? Stay here forever? Don't you have a job to get back to?"

"I retired."

My entire body tenses. I open my mouth, but nothing comes out.

"We'll talk about the options in the morning." He turns to the wall, punches the pillow a couple of times, and is softly snoring in moments. He's so at home, it's like he's moved in—or will.

Suddenly, I'm wide awake.

FOUR

Enzo Brambilla Jr. told the bartender to pour him a second whiskey—his last drink of the night, at least at this bar. The club had a strict two-drink maximum. On stage, a rigger trussed up a woman in a rope swing. Interesting, but not Enzo's preferred entertainment. A bullwhip or a cane, something that might involve a little—or a lot—of bloodshed was more his speed. A little subby with her tits out plopped her ass next to him. Tina. If she wasn't so masochistic, he couldn't have tolerated her stupidity. As it was, after months of dealing with her in an attempt to be patient, he was done playing nice.

"Hi, Master." Her breathless words, along with the rise and fall of her chest, did nothing for him.

He grabbed her neck. Her pulse fluttered under his fingertips. "Did you have permission to speak?"

She shook her head, eyes wide and dilated with arousal, mouth in an O. He should get out his dick and fill that gaping hole, but he couldn't be bothered. He'd only come to this club after discovering Amelia was a member before she disappeared. She joined right after she'd run from him. In the months after, she'd become a traitor and turned in the family for tax evasion. They'd searched for her, but every lead had been a dud. Since his father had passed a few weeks ago, there'd been no urgency from his boys to find her. It was as if his family had already forgotten his old man and the woman who killed him by putting him behind bars. Selfish bastards.

Tina had latched onto Enzo the first night he'd visited the club. She took a beating like a good little bitch, and her holes weren't bad either. He glanced over at the dungeon monitor. There were too many eyes for what he had planned. Whether he got the information that night or not, it was his last visit to this club. Far too restrictive for his tastes. "Let's get a private room."

She nodded, practically drooling with anticipation.

An involuntary sneer twitched across his lips. He blanked his face and made her crawl through the club back to the only room available—a nursery. Not Enzo's preferred choice, but who fucking cared? Any room could be used for the interrogation he had planned, even if that one did have pink and blue bunny wallpaper above the beadboard. At least the adult-sized crib looked something like a cage. But the changing table would never be used by him. He didn't get into that Daddy Dom crap. Subs were for submitting to his needs. His desires. His pleasure.

As soon as the door shut, he ordered, "Strip."

Tina was as naked as the day she was born in seconds.

Enzo reached out and pinched her nipple hard. "You showing your goods to everyone in the club?"

"I? No? Uh..."

Like he actually cared. He twisted until her knees went weak, and she sagged, her sad little titty stretched out. "You fucking everyone in this club, *baby?*"

"No, Master." She panted.

He released his grip, her reward because he could tell she told the truth. Hell, every other Dom in the place was so caught up with "safe, sane, and consensual" negotiations and other bullshit that they'd never meet her masochistic needs. Good thing she'd found him. Even if she didn't know his real name or who he was. No one there did, except the guy who had provided the required reference in exchange for continuing to live. Add in the fake passport, and joining the club under a false name had been too easy. Kind of like Tina.

He handed her a bottle of lube from the changing table. "Grease your ass. I wanna fuck you, bitch."

She took the bottle and squirted a generous dollop, taking it right to her asshole.

It was his last chance to figure out what she knew. He'd been getting far too much scrutiny from the other club members. His colored contacts and other disguise elements wouldn't protect him much longer. "While I fuck you, you're gonna tell me the name of every single other Dom you've been with at this club. Whether you fucked them or not. If they so much as spanked your ass, you're gonna spill. Tell me everything about everyone here. And if I like what you have to say, I might let you suck my dick when I'm done."

Her fingers sawed in and out of her ass, her back on the rug-covered floor, knees at her ears, ass in the air so he could watch. "Thank you, Master." Such an obedient little slut.

Enzo unzipped his pants and rolled on a condom because who knew where her fuck hole had been. Well, he was about to find out. He dragged her to one end of the toy chest by her hair.

"Bend over and hold on. I don't want you fucking moving. You take it in the ass and tell me what I want to hear or..." He couldn't threaten her with a beating because she'd enjoy that. "Or the scene stops, and you'll spend the night on your knees getting nothing."

Her whimper was the perfect mood music. "Yes, Master."

That was another thing he liked about Tina. They weren't in a relationship—had never agreed to anything—but she called him Master as if he gave a fuck about her. He rammed his dick into her asshole, enjoying her bark of pain as he blasted past the tight ring of muscle. A little blood on his cock only made him happier. He bottomed out, balls slapping her juicy pussy. "Names. Now."

He used her hair as reins while he rode her tight ass, and she spilled names. Apparently, she'd only been with a few members probably because the rest were too craven to take her to the edge of her nearly nonexistent limits. Death was likely the only thing on the other side of that line, but not much else. He might take her across that line someday, but not before he knew everything she did.

"Who else? Who's put their hands on you?" He cracked her across the ass with a small leather slapper he pulled from his pocket, holding nothing back.

Her squeals of pain went straight to his balls. In his mind, it was Amelia he was hate-fucking until she cried so hard snot ran down her face and blood dripped from her asshole. His cock swelled. Fuck, he had to slow down, or he'd come too soon.

"Tyler."

That name. Enzo plowed his hips forward and back as he searched his memory of everything he'd learned about the club members. Federal agent. FBI.

He followed up with the same question he'd already asked three times. "Who does he scene with now?"

"Nobody," she squeaked. "Not since Mia left."

Enzo busted his nut at the sound of that name. Fucking *Mia.* Amelia Kincaid went by Mia. And she used to be with an FBI agent? It was too much of a coincidence not to be important. He fucked the last of his cum into the condom, then cracked Tina's ass on the other side so she'd have matching welts. When he pulled his dick out, it was still hard, thanks to his pills. "Take off the condom and suck me."

Tina swallowed his cock as soon as she had it free, licking the cum off his skin like it was the finest chocolate in the world. Enzo thrust his hips, jabbing her throat, and snatched up a handful of her hair. "Where do I find Tyler?"

Tina's eyes bulged as she tried to answer around his cock.

Enzo eased back until just the tip held her mouth open.

"Gone," she gagged out.

He tugged free. "Where?"

"Some business out of state. I heard the other Doms talking."

Enzo tossed her to the ground like the used fuck doll she was and zipped up his dick. He left the club and drove straight to his father's, no, *his* office, making several calls despite the fact it was well past midnight. His cyber guy came through in a matter of minutes. Tyler Davis, the man who topped Mia, had jetted out on a commercial flight to Denver, Colorado. It was a thin lead, but more than they'd had in months.

Although likely pulled from sleep, his boys were at the office when he arrived as expected. At least they still showed him some respect. Fewer of them to get rid of. "Amelia Kincaid might be in Colorado. Who can we get out there?"

His cousin, Francis, who preferred to go by Franco, crossed his arms. "We should let this drop, Enzo. Let sleeping dogs lie. Business is good. No court case is good. As long as there's no trial, we don't have a problem. Bodies—especially *that* girl—are only gonna bring trouble to the family."

"Family?" he asked quietly. The other men in the room stepped back, leaving Francis to face Enzo alone. Smart boys. "What the fuck do you know about family? You'd let that filthy whore get away with killing my father."

Francis might be next in line to lead the family, but he wasn't in charge and never would be. Enzo's Aunt Vera raised a fucking pussy.

"She didn't kill anyone." Francis had mistaken Enzo's quiet voice as an invitation to argue. "He had a heart atta—"

Enzo squeezed his cousin's throat closed before the words finished sliming out of the bastard's mouth. He leaned in close to his ear and whispered, "Amelia Kincaid fucking killed him. I want a man out there now. If she's anywhere in Colorado, find her and finish this." Enzo looked around the room, meeting the eyes of everyone standing there as his cousin's face turned red from lack of air. "I'm in charge of this family. We're doing this my way."

He dropped Francis, who crumpled to his knees while coughing in air.

Enzo considered kicking him.

Watery fear-filled eyes met his gaze. That was better.

"We'll take care of her," Francis croaked out.

FIVE

Tyler

I YAWN and shift on the bed—and freeze. A cloud of chestnut hair, soft as silk, covers my bare chest. Amy's leg is dangerously close to my morning wood. I've dreamed of her like this more times than I can count since meeting her, but waking up with her wrapped around me is better than I ever imagined. Although in my dreams she wasn't wearing full-length pajamas.

I pet her soft hair. Relish the heat of her pussy against my leg. Cherish this stolen moment of intimacy. But before I can release the fantasy that this could be my life and get my body under control, she's blinking her sweet brown eyes at me.

"What are you *really* doing here?"

I never figured out how to let you go.

I clench my jaw as I search for an answer that doesn't make me sound paranoid, possessive, or perverted. I'm probably all three—but in a good way.

"You could have just emailed. Pretty sure that's what my

assigned handler, Marshal Clemmons, would've done." She sits up. "Instead, you retired and got on a plane?"

She's not wrong. I left everything in St. Louis—my job, my house, my friends—for a woman. But it's *this* woman. Even in those ridiculous pink and baby blue flannel pajamas, she's stunning. Her curves call to me. She's soft, subtle, and the perfect sub. I want her under my hand once more. Under my body for the first time.

Her warm gaze locks on mine. The light in the room slowly grows, and the flecks of amber become more obvious. I'm obsessed with her. Though I've known her for years, I don't *really* know her, but I want to. Even when I visited in the past, I let her keep me at a distance. But I can't wait any longer. I want to make my wife mine, but I can't tell her all that. "I couldn't leave you out here unprotected."

She folds back the covers and swings her legs out.

"You have no idea how much risk you're in," I say to her back as she pulls clothes from what would be a coat closet in any other room. She has this entire B and B, yet she sleeps in the small attic with a basic queen bed. Does she always minimize her needs?

Her gaze stabs me when she turns. "How can I be at more risk now? The trial isn't going to happen. No one's going to jail. No one knows my name or where I am. So unless you totally suck at your job, how am I at risk?"

I scrub my hand through my hair and try to tamp down my frustration. "No matter how good I am—how good any law enforcement is—a motivated person with sufficient resources can always find a crumb. And a crumb, no matter how tiny, is all they would need to unravel any fake identity. Even with the extra layers we've added around you."

"That's a bullshit answer."

"What?" Amy is never this direct, this assertive. Has living on her own under a false identity crushed her natural submissive spirit? *Damn.* I've neglected her.

"It's not true. Despite the movies and books portraying otherwise, a witness has never been compromised under the federal US marshals program."

"You're not under their protection anymore," I remind her.

She shakes her head. "How many people have you protected as part of your job? How many were you still responsible for when you quit and walked away to come here and wrap me in cotton swaddling because I dared to act as the treasurer for a tiny organization no one has ever heard of? How many victims did you leave behind?"

"None. Just you. You are the only one I'm responsible for."

Her mouth drops open. She didn't expect that answer, but it's true.

"Because you retired." Her free hand goes to her hip. "Shouldn't you get an RV and a dog, take up fishing like a normal *old* guy?"

I smirk. She really is fighting this. "Shouldn't you be a little more concerned about being such a sassy sub? I think you know how much I like spanking your ass."

"I'm not your sub. Not your wife. And not going to fuck you." She tucks tail and darts into the bathroom before I can respond.

I never brought up fucking.

She did.

I grin. It must have been on her mind. Satisfaction motivates me to leave the bed. A few minutes later, she bursts back out fully dressed with her hair tied in a ponytail.

She slams right into my chest, and I grab that lovely mane of hair, tugging gently until she meets my gaze. "I don't have to fuck you to be your Dom or your husband. I think we've proved that."

Her pulse races, but she's not done. "I'm not anyone's sub. I left that behind in St. Louis."

"Because *I* told you to." Because the thought of anyone else's hands on her made me crazy, and it could've been a thread to find her. I wasn't completely selfish when I insisted she avoid the scene. Not entirely.

"In fact, while you're here, we should figure out how to get a divorce."

I jerk, the words slicing right through my guts. I release her hair and step back. I shouldn't be surprised or even this upset. But I am. She's already out the door before I can respond. I dig through my luggage to retrieve my toiletries and fresh clothes. I don't have to address her divorce comment. I'm in charge, and I'll protect her until I decide it's safe for me to leave. It's not about marriage or our D/s relationship. It's about her safety.

Hell, it's probably better that she's pushing me away. A real relationship would be a distraction.

Lies. I'm lying to myself.

After cleaning up, I head downstairs. Leaving her spartan attic room and descending to the second floor is like entering a completely different home. The runners over the warm wood floors and stairs look like Pendleton blankets. Oil-rubbed bronze plaques mark each of the five doors on this level with the room names, like Columbine, Lupine, and Marigold. Creamy paint reflects the warmth of the floors and complements the barnwood-framed prints of Colorado vistas and sunflower fields. It's upscale but approachable.

A single leather chair is nestled in an alcove near the landing for the stairs that lead to the ground floor. A wrought-iron reading lamp and small round table encourage guests to wait with a book or check out the view through the long, narrow window. I can only imagine the guest rooms if she's paid this much attention to the details in the hallway. I push back the thin cotton curtain. The single-story house next door has a fenced yard but no indication of a dog. No warnings will be coming from that direction.

The guests' chatter drifts up the stairs. I make my way down and find Amy in her element.

She's smiling as she sets out a feast of cut fruit, homemade muffins, and fresh-brewed coffee. Two couples sit at the enormous wooden dining table under three weathered metal drum pendants. The smell of bacon wafts in, and my mouth waters. Amy is a gracious whirlwind of activity, placing platters of food on the sideboard, filling cups, and chatting with the middle-aged couples about their plans. About the time I decide to grab a plate, Sebastian and his mom enter.

"Sit with us," Sebastian says, tucking a second muffin onto the edge of his plate.

Guilt washes over me. I should be helping Amy, but I don't know what I'd do, and she won't even meet my gaze. I follow Sebastian and his mom to a free chair. The other guests look innocent enough. Tourists dressed for fall activities in fancy hiking boots and puffy vests over long-sleeved pullovers. No Midwest, dressed-in-all-black gangsters. At least none that are obvious.

"How long have you been married?"

My coffee goes down the wrong hole, and I sputter. "What?"

Sebastian's mom tilts her head. "You and Amy are married, right?"

Get it together, Agent Davis. "Yes. Married just over three years now."

"But you don't live together?"

I got this. "We didn't because I was traveling for work, assigned to various offices as a government liaison. But I just retired, so now I can help her with this place."

"Ah." Sebastian nods. "That explains why she's planning to do some remodeling. She mentioned she's redoing all the rooms after we leave. She was worried we wouldn't be comfortable. But the Sunflower is awesome. I love staying here."

"More than with Gabe and Katherine?" His mom nudges him. There didn't seem to be any animosity around the fact that strangers basically took over raising her kid.

"As much. And way better than Florida."

His mom smiles at him, but it doesn't meet her eyes. "That's only because you don't appreciate a good beach."

"I'll take snow over sand anytime." Sebastian stuffs his mouth with a blueberry muffin.

His mom opens her mouth, closes it, and drops her gaze, a hint of red washing up her neck. The banter is clearly a conversation they've had multiple times and is coded for everything wrong in their relationship. I have to throw her a life preserver and redirect the conversation from their weathered argument. "What are you two doing today? Amy said you're going back to school soon?"

"Yep, Mom flies out Tuesday night," Sebastian replies.

"We're going to the outlets so I can get him some clothes. You're welcome to join us," his mom offers politely.

A scowl settles on Sebastian's face. "It's a long drive. And I don't really need anything."

A day of shopping sounds like torture. But the drive will give the young man and his mom time together, so I see her point. "I'm sure I'll have a honey-do list. And I still need to get my car. But you two have fun."

I quickly finish breakfast and clear our dishes.

"What are you doing?" Amy asks as I stack the scraped plates in the sink and roll up my sleeves.

"Helping my wife with our business."

She doesn't argue. Instead, she returns to the dining room.

There is a certain delight in her eye as she stacks up the cups, silverware, and everything else. It's not like I'm turning into Cinderella. The place has a dishwasher, which I quickly load. We finish at nearly the same time. Once the food is stored, dining room tidied, and guests are out the door for a day of tourism, we face off in the kitchen.

"About that divorce," she says at the same time I ask, "What's this about a remodel?"

She crosses her arms. "The rooms need to be updated. It's been three years."

It's been three years since I bought this place for her. She'd always dreamed of being a B and B owner if she wasn't a CPA. Buying this property as her husband was one of the things I could do for her. "I can help."

"You want to help me paint and replace mattresses?"

"I'm here. It's our property, *Mrs.* Davis. I think I should help."

I can see the moment she realizes divorce could mean selling this place to split the assets of the marriage. Not that I would take it from her, but she doesn't know that.

"In fact, we should probably review the books. I'd like to see the reservation software you installed. Since I'll be here, I can help with the bookings." And get an idea if any suspicious people have been guests recently. I lean back against the counter, cross my arms, and wait.

"Fine." She swipes a tendril of hair that escaped from her ponytail, and the gold band on her hand flashes in the light. "But after I clean the guest rooms."

I stand. "Perfect. I'll help. And when we finish, you can take me to retrieve my rental."

Her huff of frustration as she spins and marches out of the room has me chuckling. Changing a few sheets and scrubbing a toilet won't make me abandon her. I'm not going anywhere until I know she's safe. "We should probably talk about a long-term plan."

"What do you mean?" She hands me a stack of towels from a linen cupboard.

They smell like cedar and lavender. It's not a soft scent, not fancy, and not even unusual. But perfectly balanced and appealing. Just like Amy.

"I think we should change your identity again and hide you someplace new that not even the marshals know about." Somewhere nobody but me knows about. I follow her into a guest room. She takes the towels, her hands brushing mine.

From the bathroom, she calls out, "I'm not going anywhere." She reappears, marches past me, and plops a load of dirty towels in the hallway.

I grab her as she passes by again. The defiance in her gaze makes me consider sitting on the unmade bed to take her over my knee. It's been far too long, but I can't lose focus. "You're in danger."

"So you say."

I take a deep breath. "I'm not leaving until I know you're safe."

She wriggles out of my grip. "Then help me make this bed."

And just like that, I'm a B and B proprietor, at least until I can figure out where to stash Amy next. Once I handle her, I can figure out what to do with the rest of my life with a clear conscience. The fact that changing her situation will likely require our divorce shouldn't make me as sad as it does.

SIX

Amy

THREE LONG DAYS and three ridiculous nights of Tyler in my space, in my bed, touching me, have driven me bonkers. My body begs me to submit to him, but I refuse to go down that path. I want a real relationship, not a self-appointed handler in charge of my protection. No matter how gorgeous he is. No matter how much he insists on helping me. The sooner he moves on, the sooner I can...start dating, I guess.

I smile and wave as Sebastian leaves for the airport with his mother. He's become such an amazing young man. Not that he wasn't already when I met him on the streets of Alabaster. Tyler's hand shifts along my lower back, distracting me from my memories and imminent tears.

I spin and glare at him. "Show's over. No one here needs to believe we're a couple."

His cocky grin has me clenching my jaw. "What if I believe it? What if I want you to believe it?"

Argh. This man. I throw up my hands and retreat to my office. It's a repurposed pantry in the kitchen with a locking door holding a small desk, my laptop, a filing cabinet, and the internet router. There's no room for anything else—except he's looming in the doorway. The echo of his touch lingers just above my waistline. Right above my ass, where I know exactly how his hands feel. I miss the crack of his palm across my cheeks. He used to send all my demons flying away. But I don't have demons now. I have rooms to clean and renovate.

First, I have to get out of here, get some air and distance from Tyler. "Do you need something?"

"Ready to show me the booking software?"

"I have too many things to do today." None of these involve him wedging himself into my office to sit next to me in the tiny space behind my desk while I try to train him in software he'll never need to know.

"Can I help you clean the rooms?"

He's been helpful with the daily grind of being an innkeeper. So what? "Pick a room and set yourself up. I'm going to the hardware store to get paint and supplies."

"I can—"

"No. I need some space. Whatever room you want. You know where the linens are. Put the dirties in the basement next to the washer, and I'll deal with them when I get back."

"I should go with you."

I stand, hands on my hips. "I'll be gone one hour. You can time me, but you can't go with me."

He steps back, hands raised as if I'm pointing a gun at him. "Which room do you want to do first? I'll clear it for you."

I tell him to pick one of the three king rooms. Those are my best sellers. The email I sent to a local artist paid off, and she sent me images of paintings I can hang. I just need soft background colors to give the rooms an art gallery vibe. The new linens should be delivered in a couple of days. Snapping the elastic band around my notebook, I tuck it in my purse and pick up my keys. Tyler takes a scant step from the doorway. Once again, I barely conceal my shiver when my body brushes against his. He has to know what he's doing.

If only Katherine weren't away on her honeymoon, I'd have someone to confide in about this mess with Tyler. I've resisted texting her. She and Gabe deserve an uninterrupted getaway.

I FIND parking right outside our little hardware store, which never happens. The bricks that frame the large pane windows blend perfectly with the brick sidewalks. I adore the mid-century feel of Alabaster. Straight out of the fictional town of Mayberry, like nothing bad could happen here. I couldn't have asked for a better place to be relocated.

Right after I enter, a large man dressed in all black with his hood up shadows me to the paint chips. I pause and slip my phone from my purse, but the man keeps going past me. He's out of place in my idyllic world.

I shake my head.

I'm being paranoid.

It's all Tyler's fault.

I take my time, selecting the perfect colors that will comple-ment but not compete with the new artwork. Every so often, I catch a glimpse of the man who came in behind me. Seems like he's doing some home project, dropping a hammer in a bucket as he passes. He's probably trying to be polite, and I'm hogging the paint. I grab the final swatch, and Pete, the owner, is at my elbow.

"Miss Amy, you doin' some redecorating again?"

I smile at the older man who's become a friend over the past few years. "I am. This time for me."

"Glad to hear it. Got someone to help you?"

"Uh, yeah. My husband's in town again."

"Mm-hmm." His murmur holds complete disbelief since Tyler's never set foot in the store. I should probably bring him with me on my next visit since he seems determined to hang around. As Pete starts the paint mixing machine, my phone rings.

I don't give Katherine a chance to announce herself. "Why are you calling me? You're supposed to be relaxing and getting sexed up."

"We didn't go."

I'm surprised she's not more upset. "What happened?"

"Emergency foster. We've been so busy getting them settled. And then getting them to their relatives back East. I didn't have a second to call you."

"Oh, Katherine. What about your trip?" I check the wet paint on the first can, a pale sky blue, and nod my approval.

"Delayed. We'll get there. But what about you? How are things with your husband? Tyler, right?"

I sigh. "Good, mostly. I'm not used to having him around."

"How long is he here for? Can we meet him? The wedding was so rushed. What about dinner or something?"

It would be weird to hide my husband. "Of course. Probably after I finish the remodel. He...um...he retired. So—"

"Oh my god. That's great." Katherine is much happier about this news than I am. "You finally have someone to help you with that huge place. Why didn't you tell me he was retiring?"

"It was kind of a last-minute decision. Problem with his boss." Or the boss of a crime family, but whatever. I step around the large man again. He's clearly not a local because he doesn't know his way around the place. That and his all-black clothes. He continues to circle the aisles like a lost toddler.

"Where are you?" Katherine's voice interrupts my musing on the probable New Yorker.

"Hardware store. They're mixing my last can of paint." I check my watch. "In fact, I need to get back to the inn." Before a possessive, paranoid man comes looking for me. "I'll talk to Tyler and see when we can meet for dinner." So she can get to know my soon-to-be ex-husband.

"Gabe can help with the painting. I know he'll want to. In fact, he was a little miffed you planned to do it while we were gone. You know how he is."

I do. "I wasn't trying to keep him from helping. It's just my only window, and you're supposed to be on your honeymoon. But I'd love his help if he has a day free. Will you ask him for me?"

Katherine agrees and ends the call. She's an amazing woman and too smart. Tyler and I have to get our story straight before we meet with her when she's not distracted by her wedding. With the paint paid for and loaded in the car, I navigate the single road through town. A few tourists amble along the brick-lined walk. A part of me is worried about missing out on a month's income, but the Sunflower will get a bad reputation if I don't keep it fresh. Better to take the hit now instead of during the busy ski season.

A car bumps into me at the stop sign. What the hell? It wasn't a hit, but maybe more of a distracted roll. I look back through the rearview mirror and freeze. It's the big guy in the black hoodie from the store but with sunglasses and a cap. I can't see what he looks like. The hair on the back of my neck stands up.

I turn right without using my blinker. Will he follow?

Should I check my car for damage? I don't want to stop, so I call Tyler. He answers on the first ring.

"I think someone's following me." I can't conceal the panic in my voice.

"Who?"

"I don't know. He was in the store, then bumped my car with his at the stop sign."

"*Don't stop.* No matter what. Go to the sheriff's office now. I'll meet you there." A door slams, then Tyler hangs up.

The station isn't far, but the guy bumps me harder when I stop again. I roll through the next stop sign. No one seems to notice what's going on. I can't see a front plate from my mirror, but it could be an out-of-state car. Finally, I pull into the sheriff's parking lot. As soon as I settle in a spot, I look for the gray sedan, but it's gone. A shaky breath rattles through my chest. It might be the first one I've taken since I called Tyler.

My hands have a white-knuckle grip on the steering wheel. I close my eyes and try to catch my breath. Someone knocks on my window—I scream.

It takes me a second to recognize Tyler. I pry one hand free and tap the unlock button. He yanks the door open and envelops me, my head on his shoulder. He smells like cedar and safety.

After a few minutes, my shaking slows, and I meet his angry green eyes. "I believe you, now."

"I'm not happy I'm right." He cups my cheek. I expect him to kiss me, but he releases me and shifts out of my car. "I'll follow you back to the Sunflower."

"Aren't we going to report it?"

"And give them your name and address to add to an easily accessed database? It will only confirm that you're who they're looking for, which was the point of this confrontation. Get you to leave your car and swap information."

I don't have an argument, so I nod, and he closes my car door. I don't know if I obey the speed limit or crawl home, but I end up there. Tyler's behind me the entire way. It's comforting, but the timing is odd. Why is all of this happening now after years of nothing?

Once inside, I flick on the kettle to make myself a cup of tea. Mint, I think. "Do you want a cup of tea?"

"Sure." Tyler's staring at his phone. He presses some buttons and wanders into the great room, talking low.

Five minutes later, I'm pouring the steaming water over the tea bags when he returns.

"I asked some friends to come out and help me take care of you until we can resolve this."

"What?" I move without lifting the kettle, and hot water splashes over the counter. "Crap." I drop the kettle back on its base and dance out of the way of the water sluicing off the edge. Grabbing a hand towel, I quickly mop up the mess.

"Guys from the club. You know most of them, I think. Master Stone and Alex Craig?"

I nod. Master Stone is a fixture in the club and aptly named for his never-smiling, former military vibe. Alex is younger with a Southern drawl—a rigger but not a player.

"And a few guys who do security professionally. You may not have met them. Cade Ramos, Blake Foster, and Eliot Hughes."

"Where are they going to stay?"

"Here. They can help with the renovations and provide additional layers of security. Someone went after you today. Pretty obviously. I need to figure out who and what's going on with the Brambilla family. I'd say it's almost certain Enzo Jr. ordered this."

"Seems like overkill to have a whole team come out."

"It was the first touch. Expect it to get more intense. Stone has some friends who can help us remotely, and Eliot's guys are top-notch."

"My friend, Gabe—you met him at the wedding—could help with the renovation. And he's former military." I'm grasping at straws to keep from having a whole pack of men come out over a fender bender.

"Great. We can use his help too." Not the answer I hoped for.

I count heads. If I stick to the plan of renovating my rooms, even one at a time, Tyler will have to room with me. I glance at the ceiling. Does God have it out for me? I can't think of what I did to deserve this complicated life. I could just run away. Change my name and go into hiding somewhere like Alaska, or Argentina, or Antarctica. I glance at Tyler, all puffed up with arms crossed. One "agent jacket" away from when he'd walked into the conference room when I reported what the Brambillas were doing. The agent in charge had introduced him as the victim specialist. Neither of us admitted to knowing each other already. In fact, it had been a bit comforting to have a familiar face on my side. But if I follow my impulse and run now, he'll chase me to the ends of the earth.

And then I'd have two crazy men after me.

I pull the tea bag and blow across the surface of my cup. Maybe I overreacted, and the guy was just a bad driver? Maybe it has nothing to do with the Brambillas, and he was just another con man? Maybe I'm lying to myself. Even if it was all a misunderstanding today, I'll let Tyler run this big operation to make sure I'm safe, then he'll let me go, and I can get on with my life, free of looking over my shoulder or lying about who I am. Free to find someone to have a real relationship with before my life passes me by.

SEVEN

Tyler

I DANCE around the ball of nervous energy that goes by the name Amy.

She thrusts a paint can at me with a church key. "Find the paint trays. They're here somewhere."

The pile of rollers, brushes, cloths, and extension poles probably hides the metal pans. She flits around, moving things from one pile to another on the bare mattress, acting like a caffeinated butterfly, not the cool CPA I know. The attack affected her more than she admitted.

"We need to move all this furniture. Get it covered. Take that end of the dresser." She points.

She needs a good spanking to let go of all the tension and reground herself—or let me ground her, bring her back to earth, and release all the anxiety. But if I suggest that, she'll come unhinged, worsening the situation. Instead, I stifle my inner Dom and follow her commands. I put down the paint she's already forgotten and help her shove furniture to the center of the Lupine room, covering the rustic wood pieces with drop cloths in preparation for paint.

Her phone rings, and she startles. "Hello? Uh. Sunflower B and B. How can I help you?"

Her recovery is quick, but she's off her game. I ache to help her beyond pointless redecorating. The rooms are nice already.

"No, I'm sorry. I don't have any rooms available for those dates, but I hope I can host you in the future." She's quiet, listening. "You might try the Alabaster B and B site. A-B-B-Association dot org. Several inns are linked there." She pauses, so polite to people who aren't her guests. "My pleasure." She ends the call. "Sorry. Give me a minute, and I'll be able to focus."

Not likely.

She doesn't wait for an answer before she taps her phone and records a new message about the inn being closed for renovations for the next thirty days and to please check her website for availability.

"You're busy."

She lifts her gaze from her phone, wide-eyed and still lost in the customer service fog. "I have a lot of repeat visitors and word of mouth. That, along with Katherine's redo of my website, and I've—*we've* got phenomenal occupancy rates for not being directly in Aspen."

I adore the way her chest puffs a bit. She's proud of what she's done here, and she should be. "I was shocked when you told me this had been your dream. I worried you wouldn't find the reality as rewarding as the fantasy."

"It's more work than I planned, but I do love it. I get the nicest people here. I think because I'm not in Aspen. Their clientele is a bit more demanding."

"Rates are a lot higher too." Along with property costs, and there was no way I could relocate her to a busy tourist location where she might be discovered. Running an inn was already a risk. Alabaster was the best I could do, but she's made it work.

"True." Amy laughs for the first time since I've been here. Her eyes crinkle, and her lips part. She's radiance and light. In a second, her face shifts back to serious, and I miss her smile. "You and the guys have to be out of here by the time I reopen. It's my busiest season, so I make most of my money during those four months."

"We'll go when I know you're safe and not a moment before. If you need money, I can cover you." Even though she's only asked for help when she reported the Brambillas. Never since.

"It's not just the money. This is what I do. I've already given up one career for these creeps."

Better a career than her life. After that scare with the car, she has to know.

"I have friends again. I'm finally feeling comfortable in my life."

Getting comfortable is the problem. The situation is more dangerous than ever. Something I need to remember because the more time I spend with her, the easier it is to see our future together. But I'm not a part of the future she agreed to. Not really. Even if she said I do, she didn't mean it. I have to change the subject before I say something I regret. "The walls aren't going to paint themselves."

"Right." She turns her back, giving me a view of her sweet peach of an ass.

The jeans hug her cheeks. I've never been envious of denim until now. My palm itches to turn her ass red again. I want to pull those old paint-splattered pants down and leave my mark on her. To make her aware of me the same way I'm aware of her.

Not happening.

I shake out another cloth, covering the bare floor to minimize the potential mess.

WITH TWO COATS of pale yellow paint over a coat of primer, the room is bland. I don't want to criticize, but the warm olive color she had in here before was better. What do I know about decor, though? "How were you going to do all this yourself?"

My back is barking. I keep myself in good shape by running and working out, but keeping up with Amy might kill me.

"It would have taken longer, but I have my ways." She winks at me. "Ready for lunch?"

And a massage therapist and a hot tub. I nod and follow her to the kitchen.

The sandwich break is over too quickly. I help with cleanup, hoping the next thing on the agenda is a nap. It's late afternoon, though, so I ask, "Are we moving the bed and furniture back now?"

"No. We're done for today. I'm actually ahead of schedule since you're helping."

I feel a little better about myself and feeling out of shape after hearing that. And I'd like to see the spreadsheet I'm sure she has with all of the tasks meted out so she can track the project to the minute.

"The new bedding won't be in for a few days. And the artist I'm featuring isn't supposed to deliver the art until the end of the month. I have some work on the computer—"

"Great. Sounds like we have time for you to show me the reservation system."

Amy wrinkles her brow. "Sure."

I follow her into the tiny office that must have been built as a pantry or broom closet. No windows, no doors, just a small desk with a wheeled office chair. Her laptop is angled and open. A wall calendar from the local hardware store has an image of golden-leafed trees next to a river. A single two-drawer file cabinet occupies the corner opposite the desk. There's barely enough room for me to stand by her chair. Once again, she shortchanges herself by limiting the space she occupies in the house. It's three stories, over three thousand square feet, not including the basement, and she's living and working in fewer than six hundred of it.

I should have paid more attention during my previous visits, but they were selfish. She was in the program. Protected. I could come out for a few days, see her, and take her to lunch. I didn't even stay here since she was always booked by the time I knew I was coming. I let her avoid me. Avoid us. But not anymore.

"So this is the application that runs the inn." She double-clicks her wireless mouse and brings up a login screen.

I place my hand on the far edge of her seat back, embracing her without a touch, and lean forward. Even though we've been working hard, she smells sweet, like honey and lavender. I drop my nose nearly to her hair to breathe her in. She shifts in her chair, explaining how to log in. She talks fast, trying to distract me, showing me the calendar and how it's currently blocked off for new bookings. The ledger tracks her receipts and expenses. She enters the cost of her paint supplies while I resist the urge to caress her shoulder or tug her ponytail.

The database of her past visitors distracts me from visions of how I could dominate her in this small space. She has details on their addresses, dates of their visits, and a place for notes. She updates the files for her most recent guests. I'll be digging into this part of the application.

She spins in her chair, forcing me to take a step back. "That's it. Pretty simple."

"Looks like." I grin at her slight breathlessness and pink cheeks.

She stands, expecting I'll move, but I let her invade my personal space—the closer, the better. I reach up to touch her cheek, but she ducks under my arm, darting for the door.

I follow closely. As we cross into the kitchen, the front door creaks open. I tug Amy behind me, reaching my holster at the small of my back. "Why wasn't that door locked?"

"Don't growl at me. I never lock it during the day."

I'll address that after I neutralize the threat.

I motion for her to stay back as I race to the end of the galley kitchen that opens to the great room. Amy's right behind me, begging for a spanking.

"Hi, honey, I'm home."

I'd recognize that drawl anywhere. "Alex?"

I breathe and tuck my pistol away. In the entry are Stone, Alex, Eliot, Blake, and Cade, luggage piled to the side.

"Why wasn't the door locked?" Stone levels a frosty glare in my direction as if I hadn't had the same question.

"Because," Amy pipes up, "this is my business. And businesses usually have their doors unlocked."

Stone raises an eyebrow. I nod my approval and take a step back. As the de facto leader of our group, I have no problem letting Stone address this issue with my defiant "wife." Maybe Amy will listen if two of us are telling her. Stone slowly walks right up to where she stands, her arms crossed. He seems to grow, and she shrinks.

"Business is closed." Stone leans forward so they're nearly nose to nose. "Lock the door."

Alex flips the deadbolt and rests against the door, his faded-denim-clad legs crossed, ready to enjoy the show. One corner of his mouth lifts in a slight smile when he catches my eye.

"Unless and until that man," Stone points at me, "says the threat is over, you will act like your life is in danger because it is. Otherwise, I—and these men—wouldn't have been on a plane at o'dark thirty to protect your ass."

Amy's arms are at her sides, and she's blinking fast.

Fuck. Too much.

Stone's gonna make her cry. I drop my arm over her shoulder and pull her in close. "She understands." I lock my gaze on her. "Don't you?"

She nods, and I raise my eyebrows.

"Yes, Sir."

"Good girl."

Stone nods, seemingly satisfied with our exchange.

Amy sniffs and frees herself from my hold. Her spine lengthens, her shoulders go back, and she pastes on a sweet smile she can't possibly be feeling. She literally shifts into innkeeper mode. "I have four rooms available right now. So a couple of you will have to share. There are two king beds, a queen, and a room with two single beds. But they all have their own en suite bathroom."

"I don't mind sharing with Cade." Blake nudges his buddy, giving him a saucy grin.

If Amy knew how much these guys *share*, she wouldn't have any concerns.

"I'll take one of the kings," Eliot says.

Stone calls dibs on the other king, and Alex grabs the queen.

"Tyler, can you show them to their rooms?" Amy's tone is soft and friendly.

I nod. I'd love to take a shower first, but they've come all this way to help me handle this threat, so there's no point in delaying. "I'll let you get settled. We can meet down here in twenty?"

The guys grab their bags, and I head for the stairs.

"I'll turn on the kettle," Amy calls to our backs. "Get some snacks. I think I have some muffins from this morning. I can put on coffee. I'm sorry I don't have any liquor."

"Water would be great," Eliot replies from the lowest step. "Don't worry about alcohol. We need to be alert."

"Right, of course." Amy retreats into the kitchen.

After pointing out their rooms, I head back downstairs. Amy's still hiding in the kitchen. I could offer to help, but she probably needs some space. Instead, I drop onto one of the couches, shifting a throw pillow out of the way, and wait.

Big windows make up the back wall of the large room set up for guests to relax, play games, or whatever. Mountains covered in ponderosa pines and other evergreens fill the distant view. A sweet garden dotted with a couple of sets of Adirondack chairs invites Amy's guests to hang out and enjoy the mountain air. Her deck is outfitted for alfresco dining, complete with a covered grill. She's created a beautiful retreat. A wistfulness drifts through me. I could see myself living here with her as a real couple, free of the threat of violence. Too bad that's not reality.

Before long, the guys jog down the stairs. Stone takes the single armchair. Alex sits at the other end of my couch. The security trio files in last and fills the other couch.

"Thanks for flying out." I scrub my hand through my hair. "I should have a plan, but I can't think straight when it comes to her. I know you guys can't stay out here forever, but I'm not sure how to shut this down. It's possible they never would have found her if I hadn't come out first. I-I just don't know." Once again, the law of unintended consequences might be rearing its ugly head. "I'm second-guessing—"

Eliot holds up his hand to stop me. "Better to bring this to a head. We know someone is after her but not willing to make an obvious execution. The tap-and-stop method is a lot more subtle than I would have expected. This tells me they've likely outsourced the hit or assigned it to someone low level. Maybe they aren't sure they have the right person."

"Well, if they're watching this place, they might be more confident now after seeing all of you arrive. You'd pass for a SEAL team." I glance out at the backyard.

Eliot tilts his head to concede my point. "Aside from the unlocked front door, we've got a lot of windows on this place, especially in the rear. There's a road beyond the back fence where someone could keep eyes on this place without trespassing. Any cameras? Security system?"

"Not that I know of." I shift in my seat. I should never have bought this place sight unseen. The pictures on the listing didn't capture how exposed Amy would be.

"Yeah, I didn't spot any equipment," Blake, the electronics specialist of the group, adds.

"That's the first thing we should fix," Eliot says. "Along with adding a security door on the front."

"I can help with the installs," Alex offers. I've seen some of his handiwork. The man could build a house from the ground up without a plan, and it would be perfect.

I nod, accepting his offer. I should have been the one to do all these security upgrades during my past visits. But I let her talk me out of it, knowing the protection program would keep her safe. Too bad I can't go back in time because I would do things differently.

Amy comes into the room with a tray she places on the coffee table. The guys grab water bottles. "I'm not sure I want a security system or doors. I have guests who return late. I don't want to give them the impression they're not safe."

"Most of your guests probably have home security systems," Eliot responds. "They likely wonder why you don't. The system we'll install can be set up to use temporary expiring codes. You can issue them for the length of the stay using the application we'll install on your computer."

"That's all fine, but the only way to resolve this situation for good is to find out who's behind the threat and eliminate it." Stone's voice is low and commanding. "We're here now, so that should be the focus. Not that we shouldn't fix her security posture, but we can't wait for this guy to come to us. What do we know?"

"Not enough." I rub my hands along my thighs to keep from balling them into fists. "Big guy with dark hair. Driving a gray sedan with no front plate. Amy didn't see his face."

"He was in the hardware store. I guess he followed me from here?" She shivers, and I hold my hand out to her. She settles next to me on the couch and her nearness, her trust, eases some of my guilt.

The guys go back and forth, discussing how they can find out more about this guy. They finally decide to stick close to the inn, and Amy goes nowhere alone.

"We can take turns patrolling. Make sure no one lurks nearby," says Cade.

"And help you finish the renovations after we get the alarm system working," Alex adds.

"With cameras." Blake crosses his arms as if someone would argue with his expertise.

"I guess I've been outvoted." Amy stands. "Does anyone want anything else? I'm not sure what to do about dinner. I wasn't expecting to feed an army."

Eliot smiles. "After we finish here, we'll hit the grocery store. We can take turns cooking."

"I don't mind. I'm happy to—"

"You cover breakfast, and let us take care of the rest," I say. I'll pay for the food for the guys, and most of them are decent with the grill.

"Fine. Does anyone need anything? I'm getting a cup of tea." The guys decline, and she retreats to the kitchen—her safe space in this house.

She's clearly unhappy with having six dominant men in her home, making plans to upend her life. I'll give her a few minutes before I attempt to calm my sub, who's reluctant to surrender to being mine. Maybe she's showing better judgment than I am. This isn't the time for emotional decisions. It would be too easy for someone to end up dead or injured if I'm distracted.

EIGHT

Tyler

THE DOORBELL RINGS on the new entry system Blake and Alex installed. Amy leaps for the door, waving the image of a guy on her phone at me. "It's Gabe."

The groom from the wedding—he's younger than I remember, probably closer to Alex's age. Good-looking, with a big, friendly smile. And he's currently hugging Amy. I grit my teeth. She has the right to have friends. I'm glad she does. Especially someone clearly capable of protecting her if she needed him to. But she doesn't. I'm here. My friends are here.

"Gabe's here, Tyler," Amy announces as if I didn't notice him from where I stood in the entryway.

I stick out my hand. "Nice to see you again. Sorry about the honeymoon. Sure you want to be sucked into this reno project?"

"I'd already rescheduled my jobs since I thought I'd be traveling. Once the fosters moved out, I've been going a little stir-crazy. Besides, I owe her." Gabe nudges Amy.

She smiles up at him. "You don't owe me anything."

"Doesn't matter. Put me to work."

I'd like to. Maybe back home in St. Louis. That seems close enough. I shake off the jealousy. This is not who I am. Except around Amy, apparently. "Yeah, great. She's got me painting the guest rooms. Alex is working on—"

"Can I get a hand?" Alex's voice booms through the kitchen from the basement door.

"On it," Gabe says to Amy. He's through the kitchen door before I can get out another word.

"He's great, right?" Amy asks me. "And so in love with Katherine."

Married. My jealousy is unwarranted, but my inner caveman wants to drag Amy away by the hair and keep her all to myself. I don't have to play to that urge. I can be a modern man. Maybe. "What are we working on today?"

"I'm finishing off the Lupine room. Maybe you could help Gabe and Alex?"

An argument forms on my lips, but I haven't let her out of my sight except to go to the paint store since I got here. It's not like she's in any danger with Eliot, Cade, and Blake installing cameras on the outside of the house.

"Great idea."

Her sigh of relief confirms my suspicion that she needs some space.

"If you need anything—" we say at the same time. I laugh and give her a nod toward the stairs. She picks up a box at the bottom and starts up. I take a step to follow. I should carry that for her.

"I got it," she says without looking back.

My inner caveman and I still disagree when I head down to the basement.

After spending the day with Gabe, I can see why Amy likes him. He's a great guy. He and Alex had me acting as a carpenter's assistant, cutting wood for storage shelves. Amy has storage containers of holiday decorations down here. Everything from St. Patrick's Day to Halloween, which I'll likely be dragging upstairs soon. Gabe and Alex got into a rhythm where they worked in flow nearly without words. And I did what they told me. But I'll still be the one to show off the results to Amy.

I find her in the kitchen. "Come downstairs. You've got to see this."

"What's wrong? What happened?" She races ahead of me and down the stairs.

I double-time behind her, nearly running her over when she freezes at the bottom.

"Oh. Oh my God." Amy covers her mouth with her hands. Gabe and Alex are posed like two magazine models at opposite ends of the organized storage.

Maybe I should have sent one of them to get her.

She turns. "Did you do this?"

Her brown eyes are wide. I feel like a freaking superhero. "I helped."

She throws her arms around my neck. "Thank you."

I get what the Grinch felt when his heart grew two sizes. I wrap her in a hug. "You're welcome." A tinge of guilt runs up my spine. "But really, all I did was assist. Those two were the geniuses behind it all."

She steps out of my embrace, and I hate my honesty. But she grabs my hand, her long fingers laced through mine. "Thank you, guys. I can't tell you how long I've wanted something like this." She sweeps her arm out like a game show hostess. "All this space."

"Had to find something to keep me busy since the security door still hasn't come in." Alex wipes some nonexistent sawdust from the edge of a shelf, his cheeks slightly pink.

"Gabe, you should stay for dinner," I say. "We're grilling." I don't know where that invitation came from, but it was the right thing to do based on Amy's approving smile.

"I'll call Katherine and tell her to come over." Amy releases my hand. "You two can't eat pizza every night."

Gabe laughs and gives a thumbs-up. There must be an inside joke I don't know about, but Amy's happy, so I'm happy.

Stone grills steaks, potatoes, and asparagus to fill up all the hungry working men's bellies. After we finish, Eliot, Cade, and Blake get into a deep conversation with Gabe about some video game I've never heard of. Blake acts out blasting some monster, including facial expressions. The rest of the guys laugh and nod. Stone paces at the back fence with his phone to his ear. Amy and Katherine went inside to get dessert a few minutes ago. Alex is reclined in a lawn chair—a picture of a relaxed cowboy with his boots crossed and his hat low enough on his forehead it's almost impossible to see his closed eyes. I'm restless with Amy out of sight. I pick up my empty glass with the pretense of getting a refill.

"I really like your husband."

I pause just out of view of the kitchen, waiting to see how Amy will respond.

"I'm so glad." Not quite the passionate endorsement I hoped for from my "wife."

"How did you two meet?"

"Long story. I'll have to tell you over a glass of wine. Can you hand me those plates? Let's take this out back."

I dart back to the door as if I was just coming in. "Can I carry that out for you?"

Amy hands me the tray laden with brownies and cookies and small plates with a quizzical glance that I ignore.

"I'll get the door." Katherine moves past us.

"These look great, dear," I say for Katherine's benefit as we go through the door.

"Thanks, *honey*," Amy sasses.

Damn, I want to spank her ass. Just for fun. Because I miss it.

I set down the tray, and Blake freezes mid-animation. "Are those homemade brownies?"

He's already got two on a plate before anyone else moves.

"I love you," he tells Amy and smacks a kiss on her cheek. Anybody else would earn a deep scowl, but it's Blake. He's like a big fluffy puppy with an encyclopedic knowledge of tech gadgets. He snaps a picture of his plate with his camera. "I'm sending this to Reed. He's gonna be so jealous. Amy, how do you feel about sharing?" Blake waggles his eyebrows.

Amy laughs him off and plates up everyone's request in her hostess element. She really does enjoy taking care of people. I get it. It was the part of my job I always liked best too.

"Tyler?"

Amy's voice breaks into my reverie, and I snap back to the party. "What?"

"Brownie? Cookie? Both?"

"Cookie."

Amy hands me a plate and settles on the picnic table bench next to me. "Everyone's having a good time?"

"The best." I nudge her. "You love this, don't you? Running the inn, making people happy with baked goods and fresh linens."

"More than I dreamed." A gentle smile lights her face.

I have to find a way to make this place safe so she can stay.

But all the security in the world won't keep evil from her door if it truly wants her.

"You like Gabe," Amy says.

"He fits in surprisingly well."

She leans close. "I think he and Katherine are pretty vanilla. They don't know—"

"Got it. They won't hear it from me."

"As relaxed as you've been tonight, I never saw this side of you at the club, only the stern Dom. I could almost forget that part."

I raise an eyebrow and intensify my stare. "Maybe I should remind you."

She giggles. It's cute, but it's nerves and not an invitation because she stands and takes my empty plate.

Stone finally returns to the deck. "Hey, Amy. Did you save me a cookie?"

She hops up and puts a cookie on a plate for him.

"Thought you didn't like sweets, dude." Alex smirks.

"I don't. Except for these." Stone bites into the best chocolate chip cookie on the planet and moans as he chews.

Amy has a happy, glowing smile as she disappears back inside with Katherine.

"Who were you on the phone with?" I ask Stone.

"Few calls. Have someone looking into rentals of gray sedans."

"That's a long shot."

Stone grunts his agreement.

"What are we doing now?" Blake asks, hyped up on video-game chatter and sugar.

"Early night." Stone's phone buzzes. He checks the screen. "I have some errands to run tomorrow. And..." Stone stretches his legs in front of him. "We should find the nearest club because if we all start looking like this sad sack over here"—he hitches his thumb at me—"ain't none of us going to be worth a shit."

"Hey." I'm not that pathetic. Yet. "You guys can do what you want, but I'm in no position to start something, not even casual. Not as long as I'm here helping my...sub."

"Is she your sub?" Stone's steely gaze demands honesty.

"No." I sigh. I hate that he's seen right through me. But Amy's made it clear she's no longer interested in that role. And I'm not at all interested in a vanilla relationship with anyone. Which means that once she's safe, we're over. And until she's safe, my right hand is my new best friend.

"Are we taking Amy?" Alex asks.

"Can't leave her here." Stone frowns at Alex.

"I mean, you know, security and all." Alex crosses his arms and glances over at Blake.

Blake shrugs. "It's not like she can get attacked in a private kink club when we're all there. If anything, there's more risk here where she's expected to be."

I glance up at my friends and meet Gabe's interested gaze.

Fuck. I search for the words to explain this, a lie that would work, but I've got nothing.

Gabe raises his hands and shrugs.

He's cool with it, but Amy will never forgive me for outing her to him.

NINE

Amy

I CAN'T TAKE a step without tripping over a big bag of testosterone in jeans. They're everywhere—putting in cameras, swapping out light fixtures, adding motion detectors—and it's making me nuts. I can't step away for a second without one of them following me. Tyler's the worst of all. He should be backing me up since this is his investment, too. We shouldn't be burning through money like this.

Instead, he's taking their side. My plan for a quick refresh of paint, linens, and artwork has exploded into plumbing, tile, and even electrical upgrades. Blake's appalled at my lack of charging ports in the outlets, although I did get props for my GFCI outlets in the bathroom. I didn't bother to point out that I had to pass an inspection to even open this place.

Alex is talking about a safe room in the basement now that it's organized. A freaking safe room? I put my foot down on that one, but now he's decided—after finding out his showerhead dripped for a bit after he shut off the water—to identify every substandard piece of plumbing indoors and out. I argued that I couldn't afford to replace everything, and Tyler nudged me aside and went to Glenwood with Alex. I swear, they brought back an entire big-box hardware store.

Stone moved into the room we finished, so I'm sneaking more paint supplies into his old room that Cade and Eliot cleared out this morning. The ceiling drank up more paint than I expected.

"I told you to wait for me."

I jump about a foot and spin to glare at Tyler. "Don't sneak up on me."

He crosses the room, and I back up until I hit the far wall. He approaches, a hair from touching me, and my breath catches. The gold in his green eyes has flared into flames. Fuck, he's so goddamn attractive when he's pissed off. In a low rasp, he asks, "When are you going to learn to obey me?"

That word, *obey*, sneaks into my panties and lights me up. His words are more invitation than threat. Something is wrong with me. I should be enlightened and hate his alpha-hole tendencies when they rear their ugly head. But some part of my brain gets happy and gooey. I growl and sidestep him, ducking under his arm. "Don't hold your breath."

His hand settles on the back of my neck. "I could hold yours."

His tantalizing words are a whisper across my ear, and my lungs freeze. "Please, Sir" is on the tip of my tongue. I'm barely able to shake my head because the image that pops into my mind of his hand at the base of my throat makes my empty pussy clench.

His fingers skate down my spine, and he taps my ass. "Are you sure?"

I'm not sure of anything. I should have run when I considered the option days ago before he had backup. Before I spent so many nights sharing a bed with him. Before I forgot that I don't need a dominant lover.

"Yep." I manage to get the single word out in a convincing tone. I meet his heavy-lidded gaze. "Ready to paint?"

"I'm ready to give you whatever you need. Just ask."

So many possible requests flutter through me, leaving goose bumps behind. "Uh." I hand him a paint roller. "Walls."

I can barely lift the fork at dinner by the time we finish hours later. Alex made a smoked pork loin that's unbelievably good. But all I want to do is drag myself back to the guest room and keep working. It's like some part of me thinks that if I can complete the remodel faster, they'll leave, and I can return to my normal, boring innkeeping world. Each day without a threat to my safety makes me forget why they're here. And it makes me get even more used to their presence, their company, their friendship—and I can't allow that. Because if I get used to the nightly gatherings—practically family dinners—I'll be even more lonely than before when they go, especially when I lose Tyler.

"Did you get enough?" Tyler asks.

I glance at my mostly empty plate and nod.

"You guys are on cleanup." He helps me from the chair. "I'm taking her to bed."

"Brown chicken, brown cow," Alex sings out in a sexually suggestive tone.

Cade's and Blake's laughter follows us to the stairs. It takes my tired brain a second to translate what Alex said to bow chicka wow wow. Heat rushes over my face.

"I'd say don't do anything we wouldn't do, but that doesn't leave much to avoid," Eliot calls out after us.

I glance back. Even Stone's smiling.

Great. My love life, or lack thereof, is now the running joke. "You don't have to escort me to bed."

"I told you, you're not going anywhere alone until we know you're safe and secure." His teasing tone only adds to the insult.

I'm not a damn child. But if I stomp my foot and refuse to let him "take me to bed," I'll look and sound like one. I'm tempted to do it anyway. When I finally get to the bathroom, my shoulders scream when I try to remove my shirt. Tears run down my cheeks, not from the soreness but because of everything else. Someone is after me. I have a house full of alpha men trying to control my business—a business I built from scratch, and they are pushing me aside.

My eyelids are as heavy as the knot in my gut. I pop the button on my jeans and lower the zipper. At least I can do that much. I slide my paint-splattered pants over my hips, bending forward to push them down my calves. I lose my balance in my sad attempt to get one foot free. The room spins, then I smack my head into the door and fall to the tile with a cry of pain.

"Amy?" Tyler cracks the door open, and I gaze up at him from the floor. "Oh, baby. Let me help you."

Embarrassment gives me the energy to swipe the tears from my face. "I don't need help. I don't need anything or anyone. Just go away."

He pulls me to stand. "This shirt's old, right?"

I nod.

He flicks out his pocket knife and slices it down the front. I gasp, but he's already turning me, releasing the clasp on my old bra. Definitely not the sexy stuff I used to wear to the club. He reaches around me and turns on the water in my tiny shower, my bare back pressed to his T-shirt-covered chest. A shiver runs through me, but I'm not cold. Icy water teases my toes, and I shift the bathmat to catch the overspray.

Tyler grasps the sides of my panties, his fingers between the silky fabric and my skin. The elastic at my back is taut, threatening to snap. He bends his knees, his soft breath trailing down over my skin. His warm knuckles graze my hips and thighs. Cool air washes over my bared pussy. "Step out."

The deep, demanding timbre of his voice causes my core to clench. I lift each foot, bracing my hand on his strong shoulder. He tosses my underwear to the side and raises around me like a storm, all electricity and tension. I'm completely bare in front of him for the first time. Heat flares from my core to my neck. His shirt lands at my feet.

Wait. What's happening?

Is he getting naked too?

I give him a panicked glance.

"Just going to help you wash," he says in a low voice as if I'm a skittish kitten. "I couldn't fit in that shower with you if I tried." His gentle tone quells my discomfort a tiny bit. He's not making this weird. Well, not weirder than it already is to have my ex-Dom, the former FBI agent assigned to my case, stripping me naked to bathe me. I duck my head into the now warm spray, but it's still cooler than my face. I'm not sure what he expects.

"Turn."

I instantly obey.

His bare chest is perfectly sculpted. A tiny bit of gray highlights the dusting of light brown hair across his pecs, trailing down to his well-worn jeans strained at the zipper by his clearly hard cock. I bite my bottom lip. I've seen him like this, but not barefoot, wearing black leather instead of faded denim. I'm not sure which is sexier. Both. Either. Yes, please.

He glides a mesh ball lathered with body wash over my shoulders and down my arms. Slowly, he works his way to my breasts, circling them. I whimper from the ache that's been building for days. I can't help but react to the most attractive man I know—one who knows how to command me, dominate me exactly the way I crave—being so tender and caring for my every need. It's a fantasy. True for this single moment only.

I might be lying to myself.

His hand stops a millimeter above my pussy. "Turn around."

His voice is gruff. His cock still hard. This is affecting him just as much. He scrubs my back, kneels, and moves up my legs, nudging them apart. My breath comes in pants. I'm as wet as this shower.

Can he tell?

He stops again before touching me where I want him. With the scrubby, he glides over each globe of my ass, thoroughly cleaning every part of me while ignoring where I need him most. I bite back a command, knowing he'll only make me suffer longer.

When he grabs the shampoo and massages it into my scalp, I nearly cry with want. I'd settle for his fingers. Any orgasm I don't give myself. But he's taking his time with my hair and defusing the intensity of the ache I have for him through my entire body. I soften.

"Good girl." He turns me and tilts my head under the water, rinsing away the soap with one hand and holding me in place with the other. Finished, I expect him to turn off the water, but he's on his knees again. I reach for his bare shoulder as he lifts my foot to his thigh, opening me. Exposing me.

"I shouldn't reward you for ignoring me when I told you to wait." The breath of his words floats across my heated opening, teasing me.

It would be so easy to let him finger me or tongue me to ecstasy. I want to say yes, but if I do...

"Thinking pretty hard." He presses a chaste kiss to the top of my mound and puts my foot back on the ground. "When you're ready. When there's no hesitation, we'll come back to this. I shouldn't have pushed you. Didn't intend to." He shuts off the water and holds out a towel for me. "Come on. Let's get you tucked into bed. I'll rub your shoulders. Although I should probably spank your ass."

My pussy twitches in agreement and frustration that all of this is theory, no application. Some part of me is shocked I'm considering anything with Tyler. That part of my life ended when I blew the whistle on the Brambillas. At least I thought it was over. Now, I'm not so sure. He's offered so many times since he got here. I've craved the release he could give me more times in the past nine days than in the past three years.

Maybe it's just Tyler. I've always had to fight my attraction to him to avoid getting in too deep. And avoiding a romantic entanglement is more critical now since he's only in Colorado temporarily. I'm too tired to think about this rationally.

I let him guide me to bed. He doesn't bother with pajamas, tucking me between the sheets naked.

"Roll over."

I shift facedown, turning my head to the side. When he straddles me and presses his thumbs into my shoulders, I groan as my tense muscles fight him and then release.

"The guys found a club in Colorado Springs. Pandora. Have you been there?"

I haven't, but I won't admit I did look it up when I first got to Alabaster. The fact that it's almost four hours away made it easier to refrain. "You told me I had to leave that part of my life behind. So I did."

"Do you miss it?"

Do I? I didn't think so. Now? "I'm not sure."

"When was your last scene with someone?"

"I can't remember." Except that I can perfectly. It was with Tyler. He'd used his hand, other tools, working his way up in intensity to crop my ass. He'd teased my inner thighs. Pinched my nipples through my shirt. He'd worked me over so well, and all I wanted to do was go back to a private room and fuck the daylights out of him. If he'd asked, I would have said yes. But an altercation broke out. I heard the noise, but I was so far gone. I couldn't figure out what was happening, except that I was in his arms, drinking some water. Moments later, he walked me to my car. At the time, I thought he was done with me. Before we could meet again or talk about it, he was taking my statement about the Brambillas' tax fraud and becoming my handler. And my husband. And now, I don't know what he is to me.

He shifts off me and tugs the covers over my back.

He must suspect I'm lying about not remembering, but he probably assumes I was with someone else. I should be. I should find a nice, normal relationship with a regular guy. Except I haven't even tried. I didn't even miss dating at all until recently. Never considered breaking his "no BDSM or fetish clubs" rule. I didn't break any of his rules. Until I did. I became the treasurer for ABBA. I don't know what that means. Did I do it to get his attention?

"If they go to the club, do you want to come?" He pulls a comb through my still damp hair, working it into a single braid.

Yes. No. Reasons and wants scramble, battling over the choice, leaving my brain muddled. I can't think about this. "It's late."

"I'm going to grab a shower." He releases my hair and flicks off the bedside lamp on his way.

A pang of loss pinballs through me. It would be so much easier if I could turn off my memories and my need for him the same way.

TEN

Tyler

HOW CAN I WALK AWAY? She's naked and in bed. For the first time, the woman of my dreams, the woman who has haunted me, the woman I convinced to fake marry me so I wouldn't lose her, is right where I've always wished she would be. And I'm taking a shower—by myself—to jack off. If I don't relieve the pressure, I'll go crazy. Her pussy was open before me, slick with her cream. All I had to do was lean forward and lick that sacred space.

She would have let me.

But the doubt that ran across her expression killed any illusion of consent.

We aren't intimate. Never have been beyond scenes at the club. But fuck, I want her.

I squeeze my cock with a soapy hand and stroke, imagining Amy riding me so perfectly. Or I could slide in from behind, her sweet pussy pulling me deeper as I paint my handprints across her heart-shaped ass. Her yelps and moans begging my balls to fill her until my cum spills down her creamy thighs. With one command to suck me clean, she flashes a smile, gracefully descends to her knees, and opens her willing mouth. My fantasy of her lips wrapped around my cock while her tongue dances up and down my shaft sends me racing to release. A wave of energy at the base of my spine makes me clench my ass before my legs go weak. A second later, I'm spilling all over her tiles. I slam a hand to the shower wall to keep from collapsing in my puddle of "if only."

At least now I might be able to sleep without coming on myself in the middle of the night like a schoolboy. She reduces me to wants, needs, and fantasies, and I love it. This is no different from the effect she had on me back in the day at the club. But there, we were always in sync, her gifting me her power, granting me the control that would build me up. I miss it. Have since the last time we were together. I'd thought she was ready to move forward. I'd been about to ask, to renegotiate, when some asshole had to lose his shit in the dungeon, and total chaos broke out just as Amy was coming out of subspace. The only sane thing to do was get her out of there—so I did.

That moment was the reason I convinced her marriage was the best option to hide her when everything went down. As her husband, I could buy her the Sunflower without the deal being shady or beyond explanation at work. And now, I'm here, sleeping in her bed, lying next to my wife every night, and caring for her every day. Refraining from making love to her is killing me. Years of regret over lost time isn't making this situation any easier.

With a few quick swipes of a towel, I'm dry enough. I hang it on the hook before I go back into the bedroom. I don't bother with sweats. I'd love to have her warm brown eyes gazing at me, seeing me naked for the first time. But she's deep in sleep, her face completely relaxed.

Stone's right. We should go to the club. Not because I need to be around new faces. Despite his assumptions, I wasn't bored with the old ones in St. Louis. Plenty of new members were joining all the time. The idea of doing anything with someone else felt like cheating. Total insanity—Amy and I are married on paper only. Never consummated. Never lived together. Not until now.

But my heart said "I do," even if she didn't know it.

Going to the club could get us back to where we were before she went into protection. Amy needs to submit, and I need to reassert control—remind her of the trust she had in me, remind her how close we were to having everything, and remind her of who we could still be to each other.

But if she won't go to the club with me, I'll stay home with her. In the end, the submissive always has all the power. I have to wait for her to grant it to me.

"TYLER, are we doing this or what?" Cade asks while we chow down on sandwiches.

We've been working our asses off every day this week since early in the morning until late evening. It's noon. "What are you talking about?"

"Buddy. The club." Blake nudges me. His golden boy grin promises naughty antics. No wonder men and women fall at his feet.

I glance over at Amy. Her cheeks turn pink. Shit, she's going to say no. "Well, uh, someone should stay—"

"We're going to Pandora." Stone takes the chair at the head

of the table we've automatically left empty. His stiff demeanor allows for no dissension.

"Amy?" I ask because despite Stone's command, she could still decline to go. Please say yes.

She scans the table. All six of us are staring at her like we're waiting to see if Mom agrees with Dad. What the fuck? I left my balls in St. Louis. Or at least in the shower. No, I just need to use them for something other than nutting on her tile wall. I'm not going to let six Doms bully her into doing something she doesn't want to do. "If you're not willing—"

"No." She's refusing? She wipes her fingers on her napkin. "I *want* to go. But I think they have a new member orientation —a munch—you have to attend before they let you participate in an actual event, or you know..." She shrugs. "A club night."

She knows a lot about the place for leaving the life behind.

"I've already talked to the dungeon owner and paid for our event passes. He's checking with the St. Louis club. We'll be allowed in." Stone takes a huge bite of his sandwich. Guess the matter has been settled. We're going to the club.

"We should call it a day." Eliot checks his watch. "It's a long drive. Need to leave by six at the latest."

"Good idea." Amy's agreement with Eliot tells me she's all in.

But that drive. "Should we book some rooms in Colorado Springs?"

"Done," Stone says. "I got four rooms. Figure out how to share the other three."

I love Stone, but sometimes... Four rooms and he's the only one sleeping alone. Not that I'd leave Amy in a room by herself because it wouldn't be safe. Right. Safety. Not the new addiction I have to waking up with her curled around me like she did this morning.

But as much as I want it, I'm not sure I can count on having it. When she finally woke up enough that morning to figure out where she was, with who, and wearing what, she was like a cat on a hot roof. I can't help but smile at the memory of her jumping out of bed only to realize she was naked and the way she dragged the quilt around her and hurried into the bathroom. A moment later, the door opened, and she peeked out to ask, "Can you bring me some clothes?"

Adorable.

Eliot nudges me. "Earth to Tyler."

The entire group is looking at me, and Amy is standing. "What?"

"Are you done?" she asks. Most likely for the second or third time.

"I'll help." I grab my plate and stand.

"I got the dishes. You guys clean up the construction and get us ready for Sunday when we're back at it."

"No rest for the wicked," Alex says as he saunters away.

CLUB PANDORA OCCUPIES the two subfloors of an office building. Do the lawyers and insurance salespeople know what goes on in their basement on the weekends? Of course they do. I bet some of them are members. The entrance at the back is painted black with a single purple rectangle on the metal door, a black P, the only sign of an actual business operating there.

We all clamber out of the giant SUV the guys rented when they flew in. Stone rings the doorbell and gives his name to the man who opens up. The entry is welcoming for a dungeon. Wood floors, red walls, decently lit. A curtain hangs about ten feet from the door, blocking my view of the space. After giving his name, Cade asks for the bouncer's name.

"Pierce." He presses his clipboard into the bent leg he has

on the stool. A fake relaxed pose. This guy is prepped for anything and seems to have some muscle to back it up. "Gotta check your bags."

Cade sets the bag he shares with Eliot and Blake on the table and zips it open.

Pierce clicks on a flashlight and gives it a thorough inspection.

"How long have you worked here?" Is Cade hitting on this guy? Can't he wait until he gets in the club?

"Almost a year." The guy leans back a bit. Apparently, he's not that into Cade.

"You work the door all night?" Blake asks. What are they up to?

Pierce smiles. "I'll be down later for a while."

"Cool." Blake, who has never met a stranger, gives the guy a high five.

Pierce checks our names off the list, then inspects my toy bag, the ropes Alex brought, and Amy's purse. He pulls back the curtain to reveal more of the same wood floors and crimson walls but with some glass merchandise cabinets flanking the edges. Pegboards line the walls with floggers, crops, and fetish wear on hooks.

I'm already in my leather pants as are the guys except Alex. He's always in jeans, but at least they're black instead of his usual well-worn work denim. Amy is wrapped in a coat longer than the skirt that barely covers her ass.

"Do you need a tour?" Pierce asks. "I can call someone up."

"Just point us in the right direction, and we're good." Eliot pats Pierce's shoulder as he passes into the interior.

A round table covered in a purple cloth holds a printed stack of the monthly calendar of events. Usual stuff. Orientations and demonstrations mixed in with tarot studies, craft fairs, and other non-club-type things.

Artwork with a slightly dark and maybe deviant feel but completely abstract hangs on the walls, some with little placards indicating it's for sale. Definitely not the type of stuff Amy would hang in the Sunflower based on what the artist dropped off yesterday.

In the far corner is a stand of folding chairs. The space is big enough to hold a class, so the events on the calendar make more sense. This place is very different from the club in St. Louis. They're doing brisk business based on the number of cars in the lot. I'm curious about where the actual dungeon is. So far, it feels more Ren faire than sex club.

"Lockers through there if you need them." Pierce points toward a darker hallway to the right. "Elevator at the end of the hall will take you down to the Box."

We move *en masse* down the long, wide passage. The place is a lot bigger than I realized. And the tame entry could be deceptive. None of us guys use the locker rooms, having left our personal stuff at the hotel. Amy requests a minute.

"You all go ahead," I say, leaning against the wall to the side of the ladies' room entrance.

They board the freight-sized elevator, and a hint of thumping music drifts toward me. The "Box" might be more like what I expected.

Amy emerges from the women's locker room—her purse and coat stashed—and I take her hand as we get on the elevator. I have to fight the urge not to stare at her tits in the tight top that gives a generous view of her cleavage. I grin as the elevator descends, and my anticipation builds.

She tugs the seam on my leathers. "Haven't seen these in a while. Kind of surprised you had them with you."

I've brought my gear every time I visited Colorado—wishful thinking or too indecisive to follow through. "You should talk. Didn't have a problem putting together an outfit."

"I kept it from back in the day. Not sure why. Um—" She stutters at my raised eyebrow.

I grin, letting her off the hook. "You look sexy as hell. Glad you kept the skirt."

"Glad you kept the leathers." She goes wide-eyed. "I mean of course you did. *You* didn't quit the club."

The volume on the bass rises as we go deeper into Pandora's. When the doors open, I pause to let my eyes adjust to the darker room. It's cavernous with black walls, black floors, and a black ceiling. Purple leather equipment scattered throughout the open room has spotlights directed on it. There's a sizable crowd.

I find our group already at a table on the far end with bottles of water clustered in the center. Amy's pressed against me. "Want to sit for a bit?"

She nods. I pull out a chair for her and hand her a bottle of water. I settle between her and Stone. He's deceptively relaxed in his body posture, but his eyes catalog everything. I already clocked the exits—two stairwells on opposite ends besides the elevator. Several dungeon masters monitor the areas of play. It's a good setup, and the crowd is a mix of people of all ages. It almost feels like a post-munch party.

Alex wanders toward a man with a woman tied up in knots. Literally. He's passionate about rigging.

Once Amy's shoulders have dropped from around her ears, I ask, "Do you want to walk around and check the place out?"

"Yes, Sir," she responds, and my dick twitches in my leathers. I haven't heard her submissive voice in...too long, and it's just as delicious as I remember.

I pull her chair back for her. "Stay close."

She puts her hand in mine and plasters herself to my side. I try to lie to myself and deny that I love it. It's just the environment causing her to act the way I've dreamed of. Don't care. I'll take it.

Nooks are marked off with either partial walls or tape on the floor with different equipment—a cross here, a cage there. Points of attachment are seemingly everywhere. Alex's definition of heaven. Amy pauses. I glance around. Ah, the spanking bench. I move us closer. Without blocking the other viewers or crossing the taped lines, I make sure my girl can see perfectly.

The sub tied to the bench has on a bustier and a tube skirt currently bunched around her waist. Her plump ass is a perfect rich red, and the way her skin shimmies when the paddle connects is mesmerizing. The Dom's rhythm is expertly timed with the thump of the music pounding through the Box. Amy shivers against me.

"Do you want to play?"

"Yes, Sir." Her words are barely more than a breath, but I'm tuned to her response.

"We can wait for the bench. Or I can take you over my knee at the table. Or we can use some straps and see if you can still hold position." I don't care where she wants me. I'm completely at her mercy.

"The bench?"

A surprise frisson of disappointment washes through me that she's willing to wait. But I'm appeased when the Dom sets down the paddle and unbuckles his good little sub. Tears streak her face, her bleached-blond hair sticking to the moisture. She's a beautiful mess. Exactly where I want to take Amy.

The small crowd dissipates because no one is next in line. A dungeon worker sprays a cloth and wipes down the equipment, much like what would happen at the gym. I step forward to verify the protocol for using the bench next. He confirms that it's open.

I set my toy bag on the small table next to the bench. Amy

is right behind me when I turn. I spread my stance and cross my arms. "Kneel."

She lowers into position on the floor without hesitation and with an unexpected grace for someone who's been away from the scene for years.

"Look at me." She lifts her gaze, and the reverence there sucks my breath. Fuck, I've missed this. "Let's talk about this scene. We're going to use the same rules as before. Nothing sexual, just a release for you. What do you need? My hand?"

"Yes, Sir."

"Flogger?"

She nods.

"Words."

"Yes, Sir." Her answer is so breathy it's barely more than a nod.

"Crop?"

"Yes, Sir." Good. She's not backing down. Can I push her?

"Cane?"

She hesitates. I've never used a cane on her and have rarely used a crop. She doesn't require much to go soaring. "It's okay to say no. This is about you."

"I don't want a caning. This time. Sir."

Aw fuck. *This time.* She's already thinking about next time, and I'm getting high on her gift of trusting me—now and in the future. But I have to stay focused to make sure she's taken care of. "Safe words?"

"Red, yellow, green."

I nod. She's always stuck to the basics. No "strawberry milkshake" bullshit for this practical accountant. "Anything else you want to discuss?"

"I might have to end the scene early. I'm not sure...after so long, Sir."

My shoulders reflexively go back a bit. Even though she's

unsure, she trusts me. "Let me take care of you, but use your words if you need to."

She nods, and I let her get away with silence. She's second-guessing herself. Time to move this along. "Ready?"

"Green, Sir." The gift of her permission, her power, triggers me into action.

"Get into position."

Amy shifts onto the bench. I leave her to settle while I select restraints, a small flogger, and a simple crop from my kit. My hands shake a little. It's been too many years since we've played. I can't wait to swat her sweet ass again. I place the impact tools where she can see them. I slowly run my hands up her arms and across her back, warming her slightly chilled skin. "Any soreness or injuries?"

"No, Sir."

She's relaxed into place, so I secure the first restraint around her wrist, then move to her other arm, securing it as well. Her chest rests on the padding, arms down and latched to the wood frame. Her knees are braced on the lower part of the bench. Hands and knees position, perfect for fucking her from behind, if that's what we wanted.

I want it.

So fucking bad.

But not here, not tonight. It's not what we agreed to.

I shift my attention to her ankles. The leather cuffs that will hold them in place look huge on her delicate bones. She's so strong and capable that I forget how delicately she's made. After locking her in, I step back to admire how perfect she looks, and my chest swells. She's mine—at least for now—as if we were back in St. Louis. This club isn't as fancy, but having Amy trust me with her submission again is everything I dreamed of. I run my hand up her calf to the inside of her thigh and flip her skirt up. My balls tighten. No panties.

I smack her pretty ass once. In her ear, I whisper, "Is this for me?"

"Yes, Sir."

"Are you my naughty girl?"

"Yes, Sir," she pants.

I fucking love that answer. "I should spank you for taking off your panties without my permission."

Her thighs clench. "You didn't tell me I had to."

A laugh threatens, but I force it down. God, I love her sass. It only makes me more eager to get started. "What color are you, Mia?"

She stiffens slightly.

Fuck. I'm so deep in the headspace of when we used to scene that her old club name came out automatically. I can't afford to slip like that.

"Amy. Green."

I smack her ass again, a bit harder. "How do you address me, *Amy*?"

"Sir." Not quite the submissive tone from earlier.

My fault. I rub her sweet naked globes, not diving between them to check if she's wet. Not allowed. Impact only.

I find the beat of the music and place increasingly intense swats over the entirety of her ass. Perfect placement is vital to avoid harming her. This isn't only about pain. *Smack.*

I gift her the freedom from making decisions. *Smack.*

She gifts me submission, trusting me to take her where only I can. *Smack.*

Our connection pulses between us. Sharp. Intense. Sublime.

Her peach-shaped ass ripens to a beautiful reddish tone. She jerks on the bench when I get the tender spots at the top of her thighs. I rub her heated skin, savoring her every twitch and shudder. The way my handprints linger. "Color?"

She green lights me, and I retrieve the flogger, giving my reddened palm a break, though I instantly miss the sensation of her skin rippling beneath my fingers. If I keep my hands on her a minute longer, I'll break the rules and finger that luscious pussy until she screams for real.

An ethereal quality overlays the heavy beat of the music. I use its flow to guide my arm, swinging in soft continuous circular strokes, letting the strands of the flogger graze her ass with their barely-there sting. By teasing her, I'm opening her to the next round of intensity. Her hips sway, and I realize I didn't secure the belt around her middle, but I don't want to stop. Her dance calls to me. I move to her music. The deeper we descend, the more connected I am to her every twitch. Breath. Bead of sweat. Every tear that falls. Every drop of cream that swells from between her intimate lips.

I lick mine as if I could taste her.

More, her body tells me.

More. I give her what she craves.

When the flogger has kissed every part of her skin I've planned to touch, I check in. Her eyes are closed, features soft. She's mostly gone already. "Green, Sir."

She's on the edge. I can take her beyond to the space where she'll float free. I leave the flogger on the table and select my crop. The first flicks to the fleshy part of her ass leave satisfying patches of ownership. Her slight gasps sing to me, calling me to continue. My marks on her testify to the care I provide. The care I want to deliver in all ways. If only she'll let me.

I breathe through the gaping ache in my chest that threatens to take me out of the scene.

Increasing the intensity, I fill in any bare spots, taking her skin from deep pink to red and her mind to subspace. When I move to her inner thighs, she screams out. Not in pain but in release. She fucking orgasms for me.

I'm the fucking king of the world. I drop the crop on the table and sweep her hair back to get her tear-filled eyes on me. "Color, baby?"

She smiles, then slurs out, "More, Sir. Please."

I release her wrists and legs and scoop her in my arms. Stone's there with a blanket and water, just like old times. Only better because this time, I'm not letting her go.

"I want more orgasms." Her words are barely audible as if she's speaking from a dream.

"I'll take care of you." I can't wait to get her back to the hotel. But first, I need to bring her back to earth.

Stone crosses the club to where Eliot, Cade, and Blake chat with the bouncer from earlier. Pierce? Alex is deep in a rigging scene, tying his intricate knots. No one will intrude.

My guys gather around us as Amy sips water, slowly descending from the high we shared.

"You ready to go?" Stone asks, tucking my tools away.

"We'll catch a rideshare." I don't want to end their night early, but I have to get Amy somewhere private, and I don't know this place well enough to figure out if they have private rooms or if they'll even allow a non-member access to one. "You guys stay. Have fun. I'll see you in the morning at the breakfast buffet."

Stone and Pierce follow me into the elevator, Stone carrying my bag. I leave Amy in his care when Pierce guides me into the women's lockers, where I retrieve her coat, purse, and panties. We get outside, and the ride is already pulling up.

"Glad you had a good time," Pierce says with a genuine tone. He's an instantly likable guy. I can see why Cade and Blake reached out to him.

"Text me when you get there," Stone says before he closes the car door.

We're at the hotel in minutes. I text Stone with one hand

while holding Amy with the other. She's come back to life and nuzzles against my neck. If I were a different guy, I'd be fucking her in the back seat of this stranger's car. As it is, I barely get the hotel room door closed before she drops her coat and wraps herself around me.

She presses her lips to mine. I tilt my head back. She's never kissed me. "Are you sure?"

Her lips are on mine again in a silent response, so soft, so eager, so sweet. I'm not waiting for words. I lock my arms around her and slip my tongue inside to tangle with hers. Her taste, her warmth. I'm inside her for the first time ever in such a small way—a common way—that is so far from ordinary or any other experience I've had. She clings to my shoulders. Her body sways with me in that same perfect rhythm we had on the bench. Every breath perfectly synchronized. Every tilt of her head, lick of her tongue, and shift of her lips draw me deeper into her. Heat. Passion. Demand. I skim my hands over her, touching her everywhere. Nibbling the soft flesh of her lips before diving in deeper. Sucking her in. My heart races.

She wiggles her hips. My hard cock presses against her softness, but there are too many clothes. I grip her ass, and she moans into my mouth, filling me with an insatiable ache. Can I take this further?

I'd give my eyeteeth to have her naked and under me. My hands gripping her red cheeks. My cock railing in and out of her body, fucking my wife until she releases all over me.

Amy pulls at my shirt, and I free myself from her clutches. She's hyped on endorphins from the scene. I have to be sure what's happening here is what she truly wants.

"If you want to come on my cock, strip, and get on that bed." I put all the command I own in that single sentence and hold my breath.

ELEVEN

"Drive." Enzo pointed at the windshield, and the lackey in the driver's seat pressed the gas. The flight had been long and miserable. The entire reason he came out was the dumbass next to him. Given one job, he'd fucked it up. At least the loser made it to the airport on time and had the tools Enzo had requested. He'd also found out the name Mia was using—Amy Davis—and that she'd been living in Alabaster, running a hotel called the Sunflower B and B. Something was better than nothing.

His father, Enzo Sr., always said if you can't find someone to do the job right, you gotta be willing to do it yourself. He glanced up at the vehicle's ceiling. *Well, Pops... I took your advice*, he thought.

The number he'd saved on his phone rang several times. Mia answered. "Thank you for calling the Sunflower B and B." Fucking recording. "If you're calling to book a room, we're closed for updates at this time, but please check the website. Alabaster Sunflower B and B dot com. Or if you prefer, leave a message, and I'll return your call as soon as I can. I look forward to hosting you in the near future."

The sound of her voice made his trigger finger itch. The cunt was going to pay. Enzo hung up despite the temptation to leave her a scathing message about what he planned to do to her for killing his father. That would be as dumb as his stupid grunt bumping her car and scaring her into driving to the police station. Why warn her when her gasp of surprise before he sliced her up would be music to his ears?

Enzo closed his eyes, visualizing the spray of red coating him as he gave her what she deserved.

"Where to, boss?" They were stopped at a light.

On his phone, Enzo selected the Sunflower's address and launched the navigation. "Go where *she* tells you." He put the cell in the center console.

"You got it, boss."

Enzo appreciated the respect, but it wouldn't be enough to keep the idiot around. As soon as he was no longer useful, he was gone. He closed his eyes and slipped into an alert sleep.

Hours later, they rolled to a stop. Enzo awoke immediately. The darkness hid them well, but the inn had an empty feel. No lights beyond outdoor security. A static emptiness weighted down the interior. Enzo would bet nobody was inside to hide from. Besides some standard security lighting, the place was dark, and the parking spots in front of the three-story Victorian were empty. A simple sedan awaited its owner under a carport on the far edge of the property. "Get me the plate number of that car."

Dumbass immediately hopped out of the car and sauntered along the sidewalk, a motion-detecting light popping on as he approached. Enzo's gaze darted to the front door. Nothing. His guy paused long enough to write the plate number on his palm and then beelined back. Subtle was not the guy's middle name. But if someone were watching, they would have emerged by the time he returned to the car. Enzo rolled his eyes but used the plate number to confirm it was the bitch's ride.

Still no movement around the house. The neighbor's windows glowed with blue television light. Random windows illuminated or darkened. Enzo seethed. He'd have to wait to get his hands on Mia. But that didn't mean he would leave without taking any action.

Enzo dug into the side pocket of his carry-on and grabbed a small geo-locator. He strolled up the sidewalk, crossing at the corner. He walked down the side street to look at the back access to the property. Bingo. Access and concealment from possible prying eyes of the neighbors. Another vehicle, a small white SUV, was in the back parking space. He came to the car in shadows, a rental. Not Mia's. No, hers was the sedan. Had to be. Slowly, he made his way to the carport and clipped his tracker to the undercarriage. As soon as it moved, he'd know.

A good start, but not enough. He needed to make a statement. Put some fear in that bitch and make her piss her pants before he ended her. Maybe he'd take his time killing her, make up for some of that torture she put his father through. Keep her in a cage and beat the fuck out of her until he got tired of her and finished the job. A smile teased the corners of his mouth.

He considered the large dark windows—too loud and a stray shard could be a problem. A single kick did nothing to the rear wooden door. Enzo slid his weapon from the interior pocket of his coat and attached the suppressor. The tiny *pop pop* wouldn't even register through the neighbor's double-paned windows. The shots pulverized the lock. He kicked again, satisfied when the fucker swung away from the splintered casing.

He flicked on the flashlight on his phone. Aw, so fucking cute. Little tchotchkes everywhere. A metal sunflower sculpture on the mantel and baskets with blankets rolled up in them like kindling.

All this luxury and coziness pissed him off.

He flicked out the new blade with a satisfying snick, prepared to inflict maximum damage. Not as satisfying as blood, but he'd wait. The blade would dance across her skin soon enough.

She'd been living in heaven while his father had died in hell. He should burn the place down to the motherfucking ground. He stomped through the rooms and up a set of stairs.

Hints of fresh paint and stacks of hardware and tools confirmed what she'd said in the message—under construction. He wasn't leaving until she knew he could get deep inside, right up close. Put his foot on her neck.

At the top of the stairs, he found what he'd expected. Floral scent and personal feminine touches—her room. From the bed and the clothes hanging in the tiny closet, a man was obviously staying with her. Not to mention the two used towels he found on the rack in the bathroom. Well, her little lover boy could piss his pants too. Enzo pulled the drawers from the cabinet and upended them. From the contents, he selected a single tube, uncapped it, and swiveled up the contents.

On the mirror, he scrawled, "Your next—"

The sound of sirens came through the downstairs open door. He hesitated, hand poised above the reflective glass. It was possible the warning had nothing to do with him. But it was also possible he'd triggered an alarm. That late at night, in a tiny town, he couldn't risk guessing. He raced down the stairs and out the way he came in. After he chucked the crushed lipstick in the bushes, he jogged across the street and slid into his waiting car. "Drive."

TWELVE

Amy

I TAKE A DEEP BREATH, my skin chilled with the loss of
Tyler's embrace. With my calves pressed against the hotel room
bed, I can't step away. Pulling off my clothes and accepting his
direction would be so easy. His directions are so easy to follow
in the club. My hesitation isn't about Tyler. But can I do this?
Should I?

If I bare myself to him and trust him with my body, will I
regret it? Trust isn't the issue between us. It's not even an issue
about him. It's me. I can't keep my feelings in check if I have sex.
Not that I haven't been intimate with other men. Three. Well,
three if I strip right now. My college boyfriend was missionary
vanilla and definitely not a biology major. And Enzo, unfortu-
nately. Unwillingly. Yet Tyler is nothing like Enzo.

Tyler came to Alabaster. He brought his friends and
respected my boundaries.

I blow out a breath and pull off my shirt. Tyler's green eyes blaze. He closes the distance between us. His hands settle just above the waistband of my skirt. He leans forward, and I close my eyes, ready for his kiss.

A knock pounds on the hotel room door. A squeak escapes from me. Tyler turns. I scoop up my discarded top and dart to the bathroom.

"Alarm was triggered at Sunflower. We came as soon as the alert hit our phones," Eliot's voice carries through the bathroom door.

"My phone didn't—shit. I missed it," Tyler admits.

I finger comb my hair and go out to face them. "Is it possible it's a false alarm?"

Eliot frowns. "It's possible. Blake's trying to pull up the video, but the Wi-Fi in the hotel is shit. We approved sending a patrol. But you make the call. Do we stay here, or do we head back now?"

I glance at the bed. A few more minutes and Tyler would have been balls deep inside me. Something I can't take back after it happens. Something I might be ready for, but maybe this is a sign to wait. My body is arguing to ignore the alarm. The system is brand new. It's probably a false positive. But it's the perfect opportunity to put some space between Tyler and me.

I shouldn't have sex with him unless I'm completely sure and he's completely committed. If this is a temporary, while-he's-in-town thing, I don't want any part of it. I should follow my club rule of no intimacy and make sure our terms are clear before I act. Otherwise, I might be living with a whole lot of heartache and regret. "We should return to the inn."

"I agree," Tyler says. There's no hesitation in his voice, no disappointment. Is that because he doesn't care? Or because he supports my choice? Is he relieved to have a reason to back out too?

The fact I'm not sure only reinforces my decision.

"Do you want to change before we go?" Tyler asks.

I shake my head and pull on my coat. He grabs our bags, and I follow him out of the room, ignoring the doubts that I chose correctly. If it's meant to be, there'll be another opportunity. Another right time. A better one.

The drive back seems to take twice as long as it should. Despite how late or possibly early it is, I haven't been able to sleep. The farther we drive, the more convinced I become that it's not a false alarm. I keep seeing all the guest rooms destroyed. Sick dread settles low in my stomach.

Eliot can't get in touch with the police because cell service is so spotty on these mountain roads. There are brief moments when the signal comes in, but it doesn't last long enough to complete a call. Tyler takes my hand in his and rests it on my bouncing leg. I didn't even realize I was twitching. I stop and focus out the windshield as if I can will us there faster.

When we finally get to the house, a single patrol car is out front. Nothing looks off. Alex parks. Stone is already exiting, heading for the police cruiser. I'm slow to get out of the far back seat, stiff from not moving, first from the drive to Colorado Springs, then being strapped to the spanking bench, and now the ride back. My body is not happy with me. I head toward the front door, where my ceramic pots are still cheerfully filled with mums and potato vines.

"Wait for the all clear." Tyler tugs me back toward him, preventing me from opening the front door.

Stone trots over as the patrol car pulls away. "They have pictures of all the damage."

"Damage?" I survey my inn but still don't see anything.

"Around back. And upstairs."

I grip the handle of the front door. It's still locked. Tyler takes my keys from my shaking hand. Everything's fine until I see the back door. I guess I should be happy the intruder didn't shatter one of the big windows, but the crime scene tape across the broken door rips me in two.

I beeline for the kitchen—no damage. It's a tiny bit of relief, but I'll take it. Automatically, I plug in the kettle, fill it with water, and press the button to start it. While the kettle works its magic, I take the first steps up the stairwell.

"Wait," Tyler calls after me. "Let me check it out first."

"The Sunflower is mine." Technically ours. But until recently, he's never been involved. "She's my baby, and I will see what's been done to her."

The five guest rooms are untouched. The new paint's still drying. Artwork safe. Tools set in neat piles. It doesn't make any sense. I take the first few steps to my attic hideaway. My sanctuary. A shiver runs up my spine. Something is off. There is a coldness or a scent. I don't know, but I grip the rail, forcing myself to take each step to my room.

The bed exploded. There are ribbons of bedding tangled over an eviscerated mattress. My grandmother's quilt returned to scraps. The pillows have been gutted, leaving their stuffing everywhere like a layer of foamy gore. My closet door is open. Thankfully, my clothes are still on the hangers. Tyler wraps his arm around my shoulders.

I shake him off and go to the bathroom. There is a jumble of hair clips and brushes intermingled with splatted cosmetics on the floor. I pick up a bobby pin. I haven't used bobby pins in years. I guess I had some in the drawers, lying upside down. Two black holes stare at me from the cabinet where the drawers used to live. I slowly lift my gaze to the red smear across the mirror.

Your next

I laugh. Can't stop. My knees go weak. This is insanity. I wrap my arms around my stomach and gather my control. Hysteria is an indulgence I can't afford. "Who did this?"

"We don't know. Yet." Tyler's voice is low, anger contained.

I nod and brush by him back to the gutted bedroom. "I need to get some cleansers. Garbage bags."

"Stop."

His Dom voice halts me mid-step. A rush of red clouds my vision. I spin to tell him off, but he's right there, tugging me against his chest. Holding me close. Hot tears burst out of me, searing tracks down my cheeks. He rubs my back and rocks me gently. His kindness is such a contrast to this violent attack. I shudder. "I know, baby. I got you. We're gonna take care of this. You're not alone."

His words flow over me. Platitudes I've used myself when I have an upset guest. But somehow I believe him, and his voice calms me enough to allow the tears to stop. I rest my head on his shoulder and let him hold me up. "We'll take Alex's room. Cade can bunk with Eliot. Alex'll share the single room with Blake. The guys are already moving their things and changing the sheets."

He has his phone in his hand. Texts are flying.

"Alex is leaving for Glenwood now. The store should open right about the time he gets there. You'll have a new door before you wake up for breakfast. We can deal with the rest of this afterward. Right now, you're coming to bed with me. I'm going to hold you while you sleep, and nothing—I mean nothing—will happen to you." He lifts my chin and gazes into my eyes. "Trust me?"

I nod, numb now that the shock has passed.

"Words."

"I trust you." Despite the uncertainty of him staying. He will protect me.

He drops my chin and squeezes me tighter. After a moment, I wriggle free. I can't stand to be in here after someone has violated it so horribly. Fucking monster. And whoever it is, is focused on me. There's no other explanation. It has to be the Brambillas. But this level of anger—this isn't a car bump, trying to get me to stop and make myself vulnerable. This is violent and personal.

Roiling nausea tears through my gut.

I take a slow, deep breath and let Tyler guide me downstairs. But instead of pausing on the second floor, where the guys rearrange the living space, I continue to the kitchen. The laundry can wait until the morning. From the kitchen cabinet, I select my favorite ceramic mug that I picked up at an arts and crafts fair a couple of years ago. Chamomile tea should help. I set a timer to allow the bag to steep. The scent, the process, and wrapping my hands around the warm mug calm me.

"Bed's ready for you." Tyler hovers in the doorway, speaking so softly I have to focus to hear him. "Is there anything you need from your room? I can get it. Toothbrush?"

I lift my gaze to his. "And clothes for tomorrow. And pajamas." I set the mug down. "I can get them. You don't have to."

"Let me take care of you." His pleading tone squeezes my heart.

I give a vague nod, collect my cup, and settle into a chair at the dining room table. The room is purposely cheerful and one of my favorites. I love feeding my guests, chatting about their plans for the day, and hearing their stories when they return. Will I ever have that again?

THE DINING ROOM acts as tech central, with Blake's laptop and gear set up at one end. I stand with the guys circling Blake, leaning forward, staring at his screen.

"We need more lighting. Motion activated," Alex says once we finish reviewing the video feeds.

Blake clicks the mouse and freezes on an image of a large man bent over the trunk of my car.

"I'm pretty sure that's the same guy who followed me in the hardware store, same size. Same black clothing." I'm repeating myself. But I just watched him write down my license plate from two different angles. And it wasn't the same guy who shot the lock out of the back door.

That was Enzo. I could barely spit his name out when Blake showed me the video.

I could only see part of his face in the recording, but I'd know his evil image anywhere. I'm torn between running as far and as fast as I can and fighting to protect what used to be my sanctuary. It's like two cats wrestling in my gut, slicing me apart.

I pace from room to room downstairs. The breakfast dishes are done. I should start laundry, but I don't want to go in the basement. I could work on one of the rooms upstairs, but they're all occupied. I can't think clearly enough to work in my office. The leaves falling from the trees out back have covered the lawn. I could rake them up, but I'd have to get the rake from downstairs.

A touch on my back startles me. "What?"

Tyler backs up, hands raised. "Just checking on you."

"I'm fine." I cross my arms and glare at him. "That's what you want to hear, right? Green, sir? Everything is fine. My inn was violated. Some asshole is after me. I'm surrounded by a bunch of bossy men, taking over my business, my home, my life. What could possibly be wrong? I'm fucking fine." I'm not. I'm shaking and about to go out of my mind. "I'm not the bad guy, but I'm the one in prison." I swing my arms around, showcasing my beautiful cage.

"Come here." Tyler holds his arms open.

I hesitate. But he's not the bad guy either. I step into his embrace. He holds me as I stare at the backyard, wishing none of this had ever happened. That I'd never worked for the Brambillas. But if that were the case, I wouldn't know Tyler. I'm not sure I'm ready to wish him away completely.

"Why don't you call Katherine?" I watch him in the reflection from the window. "Get out of here for a little while."

I can't believe Tyler is willing to let me out of his sight. "I should fix my room. At least help."

"No, you should let us take care of it. I'm perfectly capable of cleaning a mirror and mopping the floor."

Every time I let him do something for me, I get pulled in a little deeper. A little more dependent. A little more trusting. A little more in love. I'm nearly at the point I don't know how I'll recover when he's gone. "I don't—"

"Go to the spa or something." Tyler crosses his arms and stares down at me.

I give in and call Katherine. She instantly agrees. "She's picking me up in the next hour."

Tyler tugs me into his arms. "Good."

His heat and his strength restore me like a good cup of tea.

Since we just had pedicures for her wedding a couple of weeks ago, and with my line of work, I never bother with a manicure, Katherine and I decide to drive into Basalt. It has the same brick walkways as Alabaster, but it's more upscale. We stroll through a couple of art galleries and past a few boutiques. A fly-fishing shop is doing brisk business. A feeling of being watched prickles at my back, and I crane my neck to scan the road behind us.

Nothing obvious.

But really, what's Enzo going to do? Snatch me off the street in broad daylight with dozens of witnesses? He might be grammatically impaired, but he's smarter than that.

After inspecting a few posted menus, Katherine and I settle into a foodie bar occupying the ground floor of a two-story brick building that probably housed a dry goods shop in the early nineteen hundreds. The wood plank floors and exposed brick walls are almost mandatory decor in these parts. I can't decide if I should face the door or keep my face hidden. Katherine sits, and I take the chair with my back to half the restaurant but with a view of the street. I still can't shake the feeling of someone following me.

Katherine orders a bottle of white wine and several small plates to share. Thank god I don't have to make any decisions.

"Alright, spill. I've never seen you this upset or this quiet."

I consider my answer but get distracted when Cade, or someone who looks just like him, walks by the restaurant.

The server delivers the wine, blocking my view as he fills our glasses. As soon as he's gone, I search for Cade. Maybe it wasn't him. I hope it was, and his presence explains the crazy nerves I've had. It has to be. It's the only explanation for why Tyler let me leave. He planned for my protection. The tension in my muscles dissolves.

"Amy?"

"Huh?" I glance back at Katherine and realize I've missed part of the conversation.

"What's going on with you? The truth. You haven't been yourself since the wedding. And you're wound up like a banker on cocaine right now."

I blink at Katherine. "Did you say banker on cocaine?"

"Oh good, you're listening again. Quit avoiding the question."

I could make something up like I have for the past three years, but I'm not in the protection program anymore. Katherine is my best friend, and I need to talk to someone. I twist my wedding band. "Tyler's not really my husband. I mean, he is on paper, but it was only so—well, I don't really know why. It all happened so fast when I went into witness protection."

Katherine picks up her wine and takes a slow sip, then carefully sets the glass down. "You're in witness protection?"

The shock in her voice matches her face. Stoic Katherine is nearly at a loss for words.

"I was. As of a month or so ago, I'm not. But there's a problem..." I proceed to explain to her the basics of what happened with the Brambilla family and hint at Enzo's sadistic streak. I tell her all about what happened at the inn.

"This is Alabaster we're talking about." Katherine taps her lip with her perfectly manicured finger. "Someone had to have seen something. Whoever is doing this isn't local. Big guy— wearing all black— had to stick out like a sore thumb in the hardware store. I know I did."

I laugh. "You're not wrong."

"So maybe he's not from St. Louis, but Denver at least. And if he's not from the area, he has to be staying somewhere. Let me put out some feelers. Gabe can reach out to the people he knows. Between his construction work and my websites, we know practically every innkeeper and hotel manager in a fifty-mile radius." She fills our wineglasses with the last of the bottle. "What have you been reading? I need new recommendations. Something spicy."

This is why Katherine is my friend. She gets the information and moves on. I can't dwell on all this negative emotion. And she loves to read as much as I do. "How spicy?"

"I'm willing to go ghost pepper at this point."

"I think you'll love this one I just finished. Newer author, but it's a cozy mystery and an erotic romance all in one. It's hilarious and sexy. I love the hero, Ryder." I pull up the cover on my phone.

"Is that a dead armadillo on the road?" She's already taking note of the title.

We chat about the upcoming ski season and whether Katherine has healed enough from her injury to return. The afternoon disappears in a cloud of contentment. There's no way I'm leaving Alabaster. I can't give up my life again. This one is even better than the one I had in St. Louis.

When Katherine drops me off, Tyler is relaxing in the great room. I turn on the kettle in the kitchen and tuck my purse in my office. Cade walks in a few minutes later as I'm coming out of the kitchen with my cup. "Thanks for keeping an eye out for me."

His olive skin takes on a slightly red tint. "Any time."

Strong arms wrap around my middle. Tyler. "Thought you might be out all night."

He's teasing me. There's no way, even with Cade on protective detail, he'd let me out of his sight for that long. "Katherine had to get back. But you were right, I needed a break."

Stone comes through the door, looking windblown and staring at his phone. He glances up. "Everyone okay?"

Cade responds with a thumbs-up. Was Stone following me too?

"Let me show you what we got done." Tyler guides me up the two flights of stairs.

My room is pristine and painted a lovely pale shade of blue. It was white before and needed an update, but it wasn't a priority. My breath catches, and a fluttery warmth fills my chest. "It's beautiful. I can't believe you did all this so fast."

"That's what having a good Dom as your husband means. Someone who takes care of you. Knows what you need—mentally, emotionally, physically—not just sexually."

I don't want to cry again, not even happy tears.

He grips my shoulders, and his gaze bores into mine. "I'll always give you what you need if you'll let me."

THIRTEEN

Tyler

THE URGE TO wrap Amy in swaddling protective layers and never let her out of my sight again rides me hard. She'd hate me if I tried. Releasing my grip on her shoulders, I offer her my hand instead. "Let's go downstairs. Let the paint dry."

She holds me the entire way down. Having her in my grasp is good, but it's not enough. I want more. I ache for her.

The hallway is empty, and I close us into the Bluebell room where Alex was staying. The queen bed is perfectly made with little decorative pillows. I take the teacup from her hand, placing it on the coaster on the nightstand. When I open my arms, Amy steps into my embrace. I clutch her to me, savoring her closeness and her trust and trying desperately to push away my concerns for her safety. Does she realize how much worse these encounters could have been? If I had any doubts about retiring, they're gone now. I only wish I hadn't waited the full month because I could've been with her sooner. Now that I'm here, I don't ever want to leave. I want a thousand more nights like the one we had at Pandora.

But without the interruption afterward.

"I'm so thankful you and the guys are here for me. Hopefully, the police will find Enzo, and everything can return to normal."

"Is that what you want?" She really wants to go back to living alone? Do I fit into her version of normal?

"Of course. I love running my inn."

"What about me?" I should release her from my hold, but there's no way I can let her go. Doesn't she get it? Doesn't she feel it? This connection between us, the perfect chemistry, it's not to be taken lightly or let go of so easily. This is a once-in-a-lifetime spark.

"More than I should," she says softly.

I tilt her chin up, pulling her hips tight to mine. "More than you should what?"

She bites her lip, and I free the abused flesh with my thumb.

"I...like having you here more than I should because I know it's temporary. I'm grateful, of course, but I'm also a little scared about how fast I'm becoming dependent on you."

How can she still have doubts? How can she not see?

"It's probably because the intensity is so high with the threats to me."

Am I missing something? Is the risk falsely amplifying my feelings for her? I discard that argument. When she was in St. Louis, I wanted her so much I was willing to woo her slowly. Then everything went sideways when she had to go into protection. Marrying her was a desperate attempt to keep her when she wasn't mine. I'd planned to pick up where we left off once the trial was done. I waited too fucking long last time. I'm not letting him ruin everything again. "You know we're not going to let anything happen to you. The guys take turns patrolling the area all night. This property—you—will be guarded around the clock. I even talked to Gabe and—"

"Gabe?" She jerks her chin out of my grasp. "Why would you talk to Gabe?"

I shift my hand to her ass, a reminder to be respectful in her tone. We're not in a scene, but I don't deserve her hostility. "I had to explain to him what was happening and that you and Katherine had private protection for the day. He said he'd ask around to find out if any single men are renting rooms in the area right now."

"Katherine said they'd do that too. They know a lot of people."

"And you have a lot of people who care about you. Me, of course, but the guys are half smitten. Stone and Alex already thought the world of you before. They didn't have a clue where you went when you disappeared."

"You didn't tell them?"

"I couldn't. They didn't have a need to know. Until they did. And now they're here. For you."

"More like for you."

I stroke her beautiful hair away from her face. "Don't you see, there's almost no difference? We're a team. You and me. We belong together, and the guys see it."

"If we're going to do this." She taps her chest and then mine. "You and me. We have to be honest. No more security tails without telling me. And I want to know everything you do as soon as you know it. I won't be treated as the submissive outside the bedroom."

That's nearly a yes. "No more secrets."

I take a breath. I hadn't planned on telling her this part, but I have to keep my part of our agreement if I have any chance of a life with her. "Blake found a tracker on your car. He removed it but didn't destroy it."

She tenses.

I rub one hand up and down her back. "We're going to catch this guy and stop him."

"I hope so." She lays her head on my chest. I keep petting her. Her warmth seeps into me, tying me to her, to this place, to our future.

If everything goes the way I think it will, my wife will be safe. There's almost no chance anything will go wrong with all the resources we have working to stop Enzo and his goon. And once we're settled, we can plan mini-getaways throughout the year while we run the inn together. I can probably get some consulting gigs. Once we've neutralized this threat, it'll be smooth sailing for us. I smile at my vision of us together. Tilting her head up, I lower my mouth to hers and kiss her with every promise and plan I have for her.

Her lips part, and I take the invitation, teasing her and tasting her. Fucking her with my tongue with gentle intention. Not like how I plan to fuck her for real. I will anchor my dick so deep inside her she'll never want to move. I'll paint my hand-prints on her flesh while I coat her insides with my cum. I'll carry her through so many orgasms an ocean of cream flows between her thighs. After all of that, I'll do it all again. And again, until we are moored on the bed, no longer able to move but desperate to be tangled in each other once more. I pull free of her mouth. "I want you now. God, please say yes."

She puts a hand on my chest, and my stomach drops. She's going to turn me down. "It could ruin what we have."

"Nothing we've done so far has ruined us. If I don't bring you pleasure, if I don't give you what you need, you can safe word."

"Safe word? Really?" She gives me a doubtful look.

"I'm just saying you have all the power. One word and I'll stop. No problem. We can go back to doing scenes only at the club." I shrug like I'm not already lying to her. As if I could actually give her up. As if I wouldn't get on my knees and beg for a second chance. "Or not."

"Pretty sure that's not how these things work. Once we cross the line, we can't undo it. There's no rewind."

My gut clenches. I pushed too hard, too fast. She just had her inn violated. I'm such a stupid ass. I close my eyes and take a deep breath. I meet her gaze, prepared to let her go, no matter how much it will kill me.

She tucks a lock of hair behind her ear. "But I'm willing to take that risk if you are."

My heart jolts in my chest, racing like I've sprinted up the stairs. I take a breath and meet her eyes. "I promise no matter how this night turns out, I will always care about you as a friend first." Her Dom second. And her lover until the end of time. Even if it takes forever for me to get it right.

FOURTEEN

Amy

DID I just agree to have sex with Tyler? Fuck. No pressure. He's only the most beautiful man I've ever known, and I'm just an average woman. I pulled another gray hair last week. When we scened at the club, I was in the headspace of submitting to my Dom. This isn't the same at all. This is me, Amy, agreeing to make love to Tyler, a man I've been wildly attracted to from the first moment I saw him. I've done everything to keep him at arm's length—except that marriage thing, but that wasn't real.

Pain radiates up my ass and clears my head.

"You're thinking about this way too hard. The only thing that's hard in this scenario is my dick and the impact of my hand across your ass. Got it?"

"Yes, Sir." I love how he can wipe away everything but us. Here. Now.

He runs his fingers through my hair, gathers a handful, and

tilts my head, holding my gaze to his. "You're going to strip off every stitch of clothing for me. Yes?"

My pussy clenches at the thought of getting naked in front of him. Not for a shower when I'm falling apart, but for him, for us. I swallow. "Yes, Sir."

He releases me, taking a seat on the small ottoman in the corner. He shoots his legs out and crosses them as he leans against the wall. "Proceed."

I glance at the closed door.

"Eyes on me. It's just us."

I turn back to him. He's right. This moment is just about the two of us. But I'm not sure what to do next. It's been so long.

"Remove your shirt, baby."

The intensity of his green-eyed stare could burn the clothes from my body. But I can give him this. He's given me so much that I can please him the way he's always trying to please me. It's so easy. I don't have to guess what he wants because he tells me. I lift the hem of my shirt, exposing the flesh of my stomach, raising it to just below my breasts. Their hard points are obvious through the thin fabric. With one fluid move, I lift the shirt over my head and clutch it in one hand, waiting, letting him get his fill.

"Fold it and keep going." I savor the gruff approval in his tone.

Once the neatly folded shirt is on the corner of the bed, I reach behind my back, grabbing the clasp on my bra.

"No."

I freeze at his command, and a frisson of doubt that I'm doing this wrong sails up my spine.

"Pants first."

I toe off my flats, unbutton my jeans, and slowly slide them down my legs until I'm bent in half. Tyler groans. A spark of confidence jets through me. I step out of them and rise. I fold the denim and place the bundle on top of my shirt. I turn, clasp my hands behind my back, and face my Dom, eyes cast down. Can he see my heart pounding in anticipation of what comes next? Tyler promised me orgasms. I'm holding him to his word.

"Good girl." His voice is rough. Sexy. He feels it too, this burning connection between us. "The bra."

I reach up and release the clasp. The straps fall loose on my arms, and I clutch the cups to my breasts. Tyler's eyes lock on me. Lowering my hands, I unveil myself to him and place my bra on the pile. I resume my position with my chest jutting in his direction.

Tyler shifts on his seat, a hand going to the button on his jeans. He slides the zipper down. His hard cock strains his boxer briefs—for me. My tongue grazes my lips without conscious thought.

"Soon." Tyler presses his palm against his length. "Panties."

I tease the last of my clothes slowly down my legs and step out of them as gracefully as I can. As soon as they hit the pile, he commands me to come to him. My legs shake as I cover the few feet between us. My breasts bobble against my chest. My thighs slide with the cream that has escaped my pussy. I'm a wreck, and he hasn't even touched me.

He parts his thighs, and I step between them. For a long minute, he looks me over. Every inch of my bare skin is heated by his gaze as if he was touching me. My core aches for him to fill me. I fight the urge to fidget, to cover myself in some way.

"Beautiful." His hands, calloused from working on the Sunflower, slide up my outer thighs and graze my puffy lips. His thumb skims over my clit, and then he palms my belly. My feelings are jumbled—embarrassment, inadequacy, lust, longing.

"Sweet, sexy girl." He pinches my nipples, and I gasp. "Come here."

He tugs me down over his knee and locks me in place with his other leg. The denim is rough on my skin. "Color?"

I pant with expectation. "Green, Sir."

"Tyler. When we're at home, I want to hear my name on those lips."

"Tyler," I say on a breath.

His palm lands with a sweet sting that shoots pleasure through me. "Yes." The word erupts between my lips. Here in private, the two of us, me completely exposed makes it so different from anything we've done before.

"That's my good girl."

His approval heats me up more than the swat. I crave more of both.

"I'm gonna turn this sweet, gorgeous ass the exact shade of berry red to match those luscious lips." His hand lands again. "And then I'm gonna fuck you so good, make you come all over my cock. Tease that sweet asshole until you see stars."

My core clenches. "Yes, please. Tyler."

His swats pepper down on my flesh until I go limp in his hold, my empty pussy spasming and begging to be filled. When he rubs my cheeks, soothing the stings, I shift in his hold, hoping for more, but I'll only get what he gives me. If I'm a good girl, he'll give me everything.

His fingers part my pussy and slide in as he pinches my nipple again. Thick and warm. It's been so long, too long, since I've allowed anyone to be this close to me. He pumps in and out, my cream easing his way, stretching me. I'm so close. If he touches my clit or my asshole, I'll explode. I wiggle, willing him to give me what I need to go over the edge.

His hands are gone.

"No," I whine. I'm willing to beg.

"On your knees."

I slip off his lap and arrange myself in a perfectly submissive pose with my legs parted and hands behind my back. Please let him carry me over the edge.

He stands. Whips off his shirt. His tight abs are phenomenal. He might be ten years older than me, but he's in perfect shape. He frees himself from his jeans and underwear in one easy motion. I crane my neck slowly up, from his muscular calves to his powerful thighs to the thick cock pointing right at me. My lips tingle with anticipation.

Tyler grazes his thumb over my lips. "Open for me?"

I let my mouth relax into an O, inviting him. I have to taste him, to take him into my body. With one hand on my chin, and one hand on his cock, Tyler feeds me his length slowly but without a pause. The head glides deeper and deeper.

"Breathe."

I meet his gaze, my mouth stretched wide with his delicious cock. More. Give me more.

"Fuck, Amy. You're so fucking amazing." He shifts his hips and fucks my mouth with smooth, shallow thrusts. "So good."

His words make my chest swell. I swirl my tongue to please him the way he's given me the pleasure I've craved these past years. I bob my head, savoring his slightly salty skin. He moans and grips my hair. I crave his control while I revel in nearly taking it from him.

"I'm leading this show, baby. You just hang on." His thrusts get stronger into my throat. I fight my gag and relax. Tears stream down my cheeks. Fuck me harder. I want him to use me until he blows his cum down my throat. He tugs my hair and pulls out.

No. A mewl of disappointment escapes me.

With his dick, he taps my lips. "I'll give you what you need. Up on the bed. Hands and knees."

I forget all about my loss and assume the position. Tyler is right there, stroking his hand along the length of my spine from my neck to the sensitive spot where my ass cheeks part. I twitch with demand and lower my chest to the mattress, my cheek resting on my folded arms. He opens a condom. The insane part of me wants him to take me bare.

Quick swats land on both sides of my ass, peppering my skin up and down. "Perfect."

Begging words rush through me, but I hold them back. My submission, allowing him to control the pace, will earn the reward, not my demands. I don't wiggle my hips or lift my ass higher. I fight with all my strength to remain in position and wait. Wait for him to own me. Wait for the peace of belonging to him to roll through me. *Please* rattles through me again and again, but I press my lips closed and trust.

The head of Tyler's cock slides back and forth along my wet slit, taps my clit, and he slides the tip in.

Fuck. More. I howl, but only inside. He feels so good, and he is barely in me.

He thrusts and retreats in tiny, measured bursts, finding his way inside. Finally, he grabs my hips and thrusts hard into my slick channel. Bottoming out, he smacks his balls against my sensitive flesh. I clutch the covers and surrender to his pounding dominance. It's better than I ever imagined. *Harder.*

It's as if he hears me somehow. His intensity ratchets up. His thick cock stretches me, forming me, marking me as his.

Am I?

Am I his?

He swats my ass, and the questions float away, the doubts disappear. I'm not an empty vessel. I'm full with him. Full with exactly what he needs while he gifts me with everything. The swats are harder. My clit throbs, but I hold down my release.

He snaps his hips to my stinging flesh and yanks me tight to him. He presses his thumb to my bottom hole. "Come."

One last hard slap echoes through the bedroom.

I scream. Pleasure and pain merge and swirl with each convulsion of my pussy around his throbbing cock. I jerk against his grasp, unable to hold still. He makes it safe for me to let go. The power of our release whips my body like a raft on a roiling ocean. I'd be lost without Tyler, but he tethers me to this place, to the bed. To him.

FIFTEEN

Enzo Brambilla paused on the stairs mid-step, keys in hand, preparing to stalk his prey again. The voice of his host, an older woman whose usually shrill tones would be enough to justify killing her, whispered in the phone. Why would such a person hide what they were saying? Unless...

He took another step, and another, silently as a big cat in the jungle, not even rustling the leaves.

"He's from St. Louis, kind of a pushy guy."

Red glazed his vision. The bitch spoke of him to a stranger. What else had she said? He marched down the stairs and got right up in her face.

The woman paled. "I...I have to go."

Enzo yanked the cell phone out of her crepey hand, ended the call, and dropped the device to the floor. The crunch of the screen under his heel was a satisfying appetizer. He smiled at her gaping gaze. But he wasn't done.

RANDOM WINDOWS WERE LIT from different levels of the property. A blue TV glow filled the large backyard windows. On the second floor, two windows gleamed with warm amber tones. A woman's silhouette paused in front of the far opening. She was obviously naked. Enzo lifted his phone and snapped a picture. It'd been a few years since he'd seen Mia in her birthday suit, but he'd know that cunt anywhere. And who the fuck was in that room? That Tyler fuck? Enzo would cut his dick off, shove it in that traitorous bitch's mouth, and fuck her dead for what she'd done to his father.

He stroked his erection once, placing his fingers on the tab of his zipper. A shadow passed across his rearview mirror. He dropped his cell in the passenger seat and put the car in drive. Within blocks, he'd identified the tail. One of the vehicles that'd been parked at the Sunflower in the past few days. A large SUV.

She'd gotten herself some security, and they wanted to fucking dance. Enzo had all the moves and the local area map memorized. He pressed the accelerator and headed for the mountains. Through switchbacks on the side roads, the idiot kept following. Since the fucker wouldn't give up, Enzo had to fix the problem for good. He headed to the spot where he'd ditched his useless grunt—sheer cliff, no guardrail, barely a two-lane road.

Neither of them played at being discreet. There wasn't even an effort on his tail's part to remain hidden. Enzo laughed. The tail made it too easy. On the straightaway to the turn, he accelerated. As expected, so did his mark. Enzo swung into the oncoming lane and hit the brakes. The tail came up parallel. Enzo accelerated and spun the steering wheel hard to the right and back. The rear wheels of the tail's car slid off the road.

Enzo grinned at the panicked man's face, saddened he

couldn't grab his phone and snap a picture. He'd just have to remember the delightful image of sheer terror.

Unable to linger despite the urge, Enzo drove a little farther to the turnout and made a U-turn. He still had some cleanup to take care of. Ninety minutes later, he got the supplies he needed at the 24-hour Walmart to finish his earlier project. His mental list included canvas drop cloths, rope, work gloves. And a shovel.

SIXTEEN

Amy

POUNDING on the bedroom door jolts me awake. Where am I? Low ambient light filters in through the sheers of the Bluebell guest room window as the night with Tyler comes back to me. He's already up, slipping on his jeans commando. I pull the covers high to cover my bare chest. The illuminated numbers of the digital clock tell me it's not that late, just nearing midnight.

"Sorry to wake you." Agony ripples through Eliot's deep voice. "Blake's been in an accident. He's being taken to the hospital in Colorado Springs."

My breath catches as a weight lands on my chest. Eliot's words crash through the dozens of questions bouncing in my brain. I can't get out of bed like this. I should have put on pajamas last night. I never sleep naked for this very reason.

"Be down in five." Tyler closes the door and moves lightning fast to pick up his clothes. I follow his lead, and we're dressed in two minutes. On the way down the stairs, I finger comb my hair into a ponytail and grab a tie from my purse. I automatically start the kettle but unplug it when I realize what I've done. There's no time for tea and comfort. I grab my bag and return to the great room where the guys have gathered.

"...both cars. I'll drive Amy's. Stone, you take my rental. Stay close. Best thing we can do for Blake right now is arrive in one piece." Tyler is calm and commanding. Cade and Eliot are wrecked. Tear tracks mar Cade's cheeks, and Eliot is locked to his phone, tugging his ear.

I check the doors are locked. Alex sets the alarm as we all file out to the cars. Eliot and Tyler take the front seat of my car. Alex and I slide into the back. Four seat belts click into place, and we're on our way. Stone is behind us with Cade.

"What happened?" Tyler asks Eliot.

"Blake took patrol last night. He saw someone taking pictures from a car behind the Sunflower. He realized you and Amy were visible through the curtains. Your outlines."

Heat rushes up my cheeks. The image of me in front of the sheers, lit from behind, lodges in my throat.

"Blake called it in and said he was going to follow the guy. But then he went radio silent. His GPS on his phone was stationary right off eighty-two past Aspen. Cade called him. No answer." Eliot scrubs his hand over his head. "The phone rang a minute later. It was Blake's line, but he didn't say anything. I called 911 from my cell. Cade was trying to find the directions to Blake. Before he could finish, the police called back." Eliot chokes on the last few words.

Please, let Blake be okay.

Tyler waits silently, providing a rock-steady presence in a car filled with tension. He keeps driving the speed limit. I'm relieved we're not traveling on the same mountain road. Going through Glenwood takes a little longer but is much safer. One more day, first of October, and that treacherous route Blake was on would likely be closed. I might lose my mind if Eliot doesn't finish explaining what happened.

Eliot takes a slow, shaky breath. "Someone had already reported the accident. Blake was forced over the side of the road. The car rolled and—"

A chiming sound stops Eliot. He glances at his screen, pushes the button, and holds the cell to his ear. It's amazing the call actually came through. In another mile or so, we'll be in a dead zone. Eliot's quiet "oh fuck" sends a chill through me.

I hold back a million questions. Who is it? What's happening? And most importantly, is Blake going to be okay?

As soon as Eliot ends the call, he pounds a fist on my dashboard. "It's not looking good," he says. "They used the jaws of life to pull him from the vehicle and have him back up on the road. Medevac arrived while the cop was talking to me, so we had to hang up."

Air lifted. This is so bad. I could reassure Eliot about how good everyone at that hospital is. How it's on par with the Denver hospital in terms of level of care. But nothing will make him feel better, especially not platitudes from me. There's only one reason someone would want to hurt Blake—to kill him—me.

If I hadn't taken the stupid, unnecessary risk of becoming the treasurer for ABBA, Tyler wouldn't be here. He wouldn't have had to call his friends to protect me. All I had to do was follow the rules, and I failed. Now, a man in a helicopter is on his deathbed. A man who was on that road to ensure *my* safety while I was fucking Tyler.

What does that say about me?

I gag on my shame.

It says nothing good. Nothing about this entire situation is okay, and it might never be okay again for the grieving man in the front seat. The most important thing right now is to get Eliot to Blake's side. After that, I'll figure out how to extract myself from this situation of my own making and let these men get back to their lives. If that's possible.

SEVENTEEN

Tyler

ON ONE OF my previous visits, I once drove the goat-trail the state of Colorado calls eighty-two. There had been a mudslide outside Glenwood, so I had to. It was barely a lane-and-a-half wide in parts. An Amazon delivery truck was coming the opposite way, and I was certain I would end up in the ravine. It's the most treacherous road I've ever driven. I can see how Blake fell prey to someone determined to push him off the road.

The downside to retiring is that I have no access to search criminal databases. I should have called a former co-worker or Marshal Clemmons. I should have kept my focus on finding and stopping the threat.

Instead, I dropped my guard. Anyone could have seen us at the club. I counted on Eliot's team to keep us safe while I seduced my wife, Enzo's target. The connection I have with Amy is undeniable. Our passion eclipses every other one of my experiences. But I forgot what was at stake, and now Blake might die. Might already be dead. If I'd been awake, I would have pulled him back and insisted he not follow the guy. Hell, if I hadn't been having my wicked way with Amy's naked body, Enzo would have had nothing to take a picture of in the first place.

All tied up in Amy, in rekindling or just accelerating our relationship, I failed to consider what could happen to my friends. They dropped everything to come out to Alabaster and help me because I asked. And what did I do? I spent my time figuring out how to get inside my wife. That isn't worth Blake's life.

It occurs to me that Blake might have snapped a picture of the license plate of the car he was following. His phone is at the bottom of a cliff in a mangled car with too much of his blood. But if there's a cloud backup...I can't ask Eliot about that now. The only thing I should worry about is getting us safely to the hospital.

Then I'll get my head in the game and find the fucker or fuckers who did this. Stop the threat. Get us to a place where Amy is safe, and the guys can go home. My passion for Amy won't change, but it can't be the priority. Nothing could have made that more obvious than the events of tonight.

There's a reason the company forbids fraternizing with the witnesses. The minute I violated that sacred rule, truly fucked it sideways, everything went pear-shaped. I'm the one who shit all over that rule, but my buddy is paying the price.

Please, just let him live.

From this moment on, I will be laser-focused on finding the asshole who did this and making it as right as it can be for my brothers. Guys I brought out here to back me up to do the job, not so I could fuck Amy. From this moment forward, everything else is on hold. Even Amy. I glance in the rearview mirror and meet her sweet brown eyes. She drops her gaze.

Even she realizes I fucked up and didn't keep my team at the forefront of my focus. It's unforgivable. I manage to get us to the emergency room in one piece. The building is huge, a series of brick cylinders clamped together. It's still dark, and the parking lot has an eerie glow from lights posted sporadically. Stone pulls into an adjacent space, and we troop into the emergency room exit through the wide sliding glass doors. If I didn't know better, I'd think we were in an airport or a bank lobby. Eliot approaches the staffed window, but none of us look for a seat.

Amy says something, but I don't hear it because Eliot is coming back from talking to the staff.

"Blake's already in surgery." Eliot grips the back of his neck. "They only told me that because I'm his employer and have all his insurance information. They opened up a bit when I tugged the purse strings. But they didn't tell me anything about his condition except that it will be hours before we know anything. I explained that we are his co-workers and his family. I have a medical power of attorney in his employee file if it comes to that." Eliot crosses his arms.

"Did you explain we aren't going anywhere without him?" Cade asks.

Eliot grits out, "In little words."

"I'll find the restrooms," Stone says. "And get the Wi-Fi password. You stake out that area." Stone indicates a group of chairs set apart from the main walkway that has a view of the doors to the interior of the ER. But Blake is already in another part of this circular maze, in surgery fighting for his life.

Please, God. Please let him make it. I know I don't deserve to ask you anything. You probably don't even recognize my voice, but this is Blake I'm asking for. He's one of the best people I know, and it will break some of the other best people I know if he doesn't make it.

I have to ask. It's the only thing I have left. I haven't felt this powerless since the entire cart of chaos got set in motion with the death of Enzo Brambilla Sr.

It's time to find Junior. He came out here to do the job himself. We've been letting him come to us. I scroll through my recent calls and hit dial.

"This is Gabe." The man sounds exhausted. I check my watch and wince.

"Sorry for the extreme morning call. This is Tyler. Amy's...husband."

"No problem, I was awake. What can I do for you?" Gabe's a good guy, lying about not waking him up.

I give him the short version of what's happening. "There is one thing you can do to help."

"Name it."

"Amy said you and Katherine were asking if the local innkeepers had any big single guys staying with them."

"Yeah, nothing came out of that."

"Can you ask again, but see if any of them have any guests from Illinois? East St. Louis, to be specific. Or St. Louis, Missouri."

"I'll make the calls. The only person we haven't heard from is the former president of ABBA. The B and B association. But she's not fond of Katherine or me."

"I'm familiar with the association." Since that was the flag that spurred him to drop everything and come to Alabaster.

"Deborah, the current president, was supposed to call her yesterday, but I haven't heard back. I'll follow up in a couple of hours."

"Thanks, man, I owe you one."

"Nah, this is for Amy. She's practically family."

At least Amy has people who care about her besides just me. I pivot to find her. She's sitting, eyes closed. Alex is right next to her. Good. He can take the lead on watching her while I try to clean up the mess I've made. If that's even possible.

I take a necessary restroom break, then get the internet password from Stone. The man pops a charging cable into the outlet and lays it on the decorative table between two chairs.

"You thought of everything."

"Cade. I think he keeps a spare in his pocket at all times."

I can't work up a grin or even a positive sentiment. Instead, I do what I should have done days ago and shoot off emails to my former co-workers and Marshal Clemmons. After pacing the half-circle track multiple times, a wave of exhaustion hits me. I should have responses soon. The guys are an hour ahead of us. But it's still early, and it may take a while to get the answers to the questions I asked.

I drop into an empty seat closest to the ER doors and stretch out as best I can to grab some sleep.

I'm not sure how much time passes, but I jerk awake when Stone elbows me. "Doc's coming out."

A woman with her hair covered in a green surgery cap, a round face, and tired eyes closes the distance to us as we all stand. "You're Blake Foster's family?"

EIGHTEEN

Amy

AS SOON AS the doctor stops walking, the guys surround her in a half-circle of concern and muscles. Tyler is tense, his arms crossed when he's not dragging one of his hands through his disheveled hair. His guilt is palpable. Or maybe I'm putting my feelings on him.

"Surgery went well. He's in recovery," the doctor says. The guys pepper her with questions, and she holds up a hand. "Let me tell you what I know. If you still have questions, I'm happy to answer them."

This is a family discussion, not one I should be involved in. But there is something I can do.

I slip away and ask the person at the far desk for help. He directs me to a bank of elevators. The café is open, barely. At least the coffee will be fresh, and I can bring the guys back some sustenance. The fact that the doctor didn't ask them to take a seat tells me Blake is still fighting. I have no clue what his future will hold, but he's alive right now. No way the guys are leaving without him. They don't need me hanging around, but it's not like I can leave. They can't squish into a single vehicle for that long drive. The big SUV is probably being dragged out of the ravine after being ripped open to get Blake out. I could rent a car.

I gather the two trays of coffee stacked and the bag of pastries and protein bars and make my way back to the ER. As soon as the elevator doors open, tattooed arms reach in and take the coffees. I meet Stone's eyes and recoil. He's pissed.

"I can carry those." My words bounce off his back, unacknowledged.

He stops in front of an empty bay of chairs. "Sit."

Oh god, what's happened? I drop into the chair. He hands me a coffee and then takes the bag from me. "I can help."

"Stay there. I'll be back. We're going to have a chat, you and I."

A sudden urge to pee hits me, but it's just nerves, and I don't dare move. I've never spent much time with Stone. Even while he's been here, he's stayed busy, been on the phone or gone. Back in St. Louis, I knew who he was. Everyone knew who he was. But I never "chatted" with him. I know what he's going to say. Stone's going to tell me I need to let Tyler go. That everything that has happened has been a result of my poor choice. I brought the threat down on myself by breaking the rules.

I can't argue with him. He's crouched down in front of Eliot and Cade. Tyler has an arm around Cade, who is more upset than when I left. Apparently, the doctor's news wasn't all good.

Alex comes up behind me and sits. "Hey, Amy. How're ya holdin' up?"

How can he be asking about me? "What's happening with Blake?"

"Doc says Blake has a compression injury from the wreck. Not sure how long he was down there, but long enough, and he's got two broken legs and a back injury. They set all the bones. Took out his spleen. But he's showing signs of paralysis. Could be temporary. Could be anywhere from the upper chest down. They won't know for a while."

"But he'll be okay? I mean, he's going to make it?" I hang on the answer. He has to make it.

"Don't know. The next forty-eight hours are a big deal. They gotta watch his kidneys and make sure he doesn't get a blood infection. The next twelve hours will be the most dangerous because of being crushed in the car."

"Is there anything I can do?"

Alex doesn't say anything.

He's too polite to say I've done enough. This is horrible. The waiting will be like a razor blade cut to these guys for every minute that passes. Tears for Blake and Tyler and all of them well in my eyes. But I don't have the right to cry. I caused this. "Alex, can you point me to the restroom?"

He indicates the direction he came from, and I set my coffee down and practically run all the way there. I go to the far wall and pull out a few paper towels before I slide to the floor and let my tears take over. Sobs rack my body. Blake, that beautiful, funny surfer dude, tech wizard, is in a hospital bed fighting for his life.

For the first time, I have no idea what I'm supposed to do. I hold all of the responsibility and none of the ability to take action. When I turned in Enzo Sr., I knew what had to be done. I was prepared to testify. I've always been in control. And while it looked like everything was coming together—the inn remodel, my life in Alabaster, my relationship with Tyler—one single wrong move caused it to unravel completely. One fatal error. Except Blake's paying the price, and only God can help him now.

The door bangs open. Lug-sole booted legs stop right at my feet. I look up to find Stone glaring down at me. He grips my biceps and lifts me from the floor. "Clean your face."

I do as he says because I don't have a reason not to. I don't want to fight with anyone—especially Stone.

"Were you hiding from me?"

Maybe. "Alex knew where I went."

"Come on. We're going for a drive."

NINETEEN

Tyler

AS SOON AS we finish questioning the doctor, I huddle up with Eliot and Cade. They look like they were down in the canyon under the car that held Blake. "I'm not going to make light of the situation. From what the doctor said, he's in bad shape. But we have some positives going for us. He's relatively young, in great shape, and he has a lot to live for and tons of support."

Eliot nods, but he might be communicating with a ghost for all he's connecting.

Cade, rocking back and forth slightly, stares at me. "I need to see him."

I repeat what the doc said. "As soon as he's out of recovery and in a bed in ICU, we can go in one at a time."

"I'm not leaving this hospital until he does." Cade's tone is resolute, not that I would consider arguing with him.

"Of course not. There are plenty of us to make sure all the

bases are covered." I glance around. Alex is sitting alone. Wait. Where the fuck is Amy? If anything's happened… I wasn't paying attention. Was Alex? Did she get grabbed? "I'll be right back," I promise Eliot. I speak quietly when I ask Alex where Amy is, fighting the urge to scream and accuse him of what I've been doing—neglecting her.

"Stone took her to get some air."

The iron bands around my chest release one notch. Stone has the skills from his time in the military to keep her safe. He's aware of how much she means to me. I release the first breath since I noticed her missing. "Is she okay?"

"Are any of us?"

I settle in the empty seat next to Alex. "No, but we have to be for Blake."

"Not sure Eliot and Cade can be. Those guys do everything together. Their business…everything."

Their business, their lives, even women.

"If Blake dies or is paralyzed, dude. I mean, not that being paralyzed is a deal breaker." Alex drags a hand over his mouth. "But it's a whole different rodeo. You know?"

"I do."

"The thing is, he's going to need serious rehab and a different living situation. Accessible. I've done those renovations and know what goes into it. But a reno can only go so far. Better to design and build the space right from the get-go."

"The Sunflower doesn't have any ground-floor bedrooms." For whatever reason, I can only imagine Blake returning to the place we've been calling home. "The only bath is that half off the kitchen." Blake would need an elevator.

"You see my point. If we're staying out here like Stone's mentioned—"

The possibility sends a tiny flare of hope through me. "Stone said something about staying in Colorado?"

"Just in passing, before all this happened. I think he likes it out here. I know I do. I've hated living in St. Louis since the day I stepped off the bus." Alex wipes his palms on his jeans and arches his back. "Whole lot more room to breathe. Better air too. I can get construction work anywhere. And with all these high-dollar digs nearby, there has to be security jobs."

"I don't think Eliot or Cade are planning to work at all until Blake is back on his feet. Or at least as healed as he can get." If Blake dies... My guts twist. I can't even wrap my mind around that scenario.

"Need to at least think about how that's gonna work if he's in a chair. Not that we were all planning to live with you and Amy forever." Alex nudges me with his shoulder.

"Thank God for that." I try to make it sound light, but I'm not quite ready to joke around.

"Saw guys come back from horrible injuries on the ranch and the rodeo. It ain't over till it's over. Gotta plan like Blake's gonna walk out of here."

"After lots of rehab. Probably best to find a place to rent here in Colorado Springs. Three bedroom. Accessible."

"Yeah, 'cause even in the short term, with two busted-up legs, he's gonna be in a chair for a couple of months."

Alex is damn smart for being the youngest of all of us. As an old soul, he sees things. Thinks about life in such a practical but optimistic way. For as often as failure has cracked him in the ass, the man plans for success like no one else I know.

I stand. "I need to make some phone calls and grab some more food. That protein bar only fueled my hunger. Want me to get you something? I mean, I think one of us should stay with them."

"I'm good. I ate two of the bars and some pastry thing. My stomach feels like it might explode."

"My cell will be on." I glance at it. It's still mostly charged.

Alex shoots out his leg and digs in his pocket. "Brought a charger if you need it."

"Of course you did." I slap palms with him. "I'm good for now. Won't be gone long."

"You want me to call when Amy and Stone return?"

Another situation I need to handle besides the threat. The mess I made by having sex with her when I should've been focused on her safety. "Yeah. That'd be good."

After getting directions to the café, I move to the far corner of the eatery. Back here, I won't bother anyone with the calls I have to make. The first call is to Reed. It's the one I'm dreading, so I do it first.

"Tyler? What's going on? I haven't heard from Eliot since he told me Blake was in an accident and that he would call me when he knew more. I didn't want to interrupt, but please, tell me it's good news."

Stoic Reed knows it has to be bad news, or I wouldn't be calling. His pleading tone isn't for me. It's for whatever higher power he believes in. I can practically hear his silent begging. I swallow hard and steel myself. "We're not out of the woods, but he made it through surgery."

"That's good." Like a poker player seeing a single ace.

"Both legs were smashed up pretty good, and they had to remove his spleen."

"Dear God. What happened?"

A wave of shame engulfs me. "The goon who went after Amy? The reason for the guys coming out? We're pretty sure he ran Blake off the road into a deep crevasse. The car flipped, and Blake was crushed."

"No." The howl of denial has me tearing up. I can see Reed on his knees clutching the phone—I've delivered terrible news far too often not to anticipate the reaction. Denial. I clench my jaw and try to hold it together. No matter how bad the news is, he has to hear it. Get it all out. I set my jaw against my own breakdown.

"He's out of surgery. They have to keep him in the ICU because this type of injury can get complicated after the fact. The next"—I glance at my watch—"eleven hours are the most dangerous. Then we've got another day and a half of high risk. After that, we can work on figuring out the permanence of the possible paralysis." There, pretty much as the doctor explained it to us.

Reed is wordless, but the sobs he's choking down tear my own heart in half. I hold my own guilt and grief down. I don't deserve to fall apart. He clears his throat. "Blake's going to make it."

"He will." Please let me not be wrong. "And the doctor is optimistic that he'll make it through the next two days. But I need you to do something for your guys."

"I should have been out there with them."

This one is a huge ask. "I need you to stay there and finish the job."

"I can't not go. He's...more than a brother." Another sob from Reed rips through me.

"I know." And with every minute, I'm learning how tightly woven these guys are. "But they aren't working. You're the only one bringing in any income to the business. I'll figure out how to cover the medical insurance payments for the next six months. I owe them for everything they've done out here. I should have set it up as a paid job in the first place."

"You're family." He pauses to take a ragged breath. "We don't charge family."

I choke on his easy acceptance. Not an ounce of anger for what I let happen. I don't deserve it. "And I'm taking care of my family by paying the insurance. But they're going to need help with the property and the business. They need you in St. Louis to keep running things."

"You're right. I know you're right. But I fucking hate it. I feel like I'm failing him."

"Sometimes the best thing we can do for someone we love is to take care of the details they can't, even if it keeps you apart. It's still love." I hope Amy will understand when I do what I have to in order to keep her safe.

"You're not wrong, but will the people we love recognize that sacrifice or just see it as abandonment?"

"It's not abandonment. It's prioritizing their needs over our wants. That's what we do for people who matter."

"I love him," Reed says, the words like a prayer.

I've never heard them say it, not in public at least. But all four of them are closer than any couple I know. "When is this contract up?"

He blows out a breath. "I just agreed to stay until the end of the year."

"So a little over ninety days. We'll get you out here to see him before that. But there's no point in you flying out to sit in the waiting room."

"Don't let him die before I see him again."

Reed isn't talking to me, but the words land like a weight on my chest. I finish the call and set my phone on the table. Wiping the tears from my eyes, I pray I never have to call Reed with worse news.

TWENTY

Amy

I REST my head against the passenger window and watch the sunrise. Stone's quiet presence fills the car. He found a park, and we've just been sitting here. The tension inside hasn't eased at all.

"You have to make a choice."

I lift my head and meet his gaze. "About what?"

"You've got Tyler tied up in knots. He's all in one moment and pulling back the next, unsure where he stands. That's on you. If you can't fully commit, you need to cut ties now before he really gets hurt."

"But I—"

"Listen."

I close my mouth in response to the stern command. This is not the friendly, stoic man who's been staying at the Sunflower for the past weeks. I try to shrink into the seat without success.

"I've watched Tyler spend the past few years doing everything he can to keep you safe. He hasn't talked about you at all, but that alone told me how critical it was to keep you hidden and secure. Every vacation day he's been able to take has been to go to Colorado. He doesn't ski." Somehow, his steely gaze gets more intense.

I wish I were as small as I feel right now. "I had no idea."

"He did everything he could, and you blew it. He asked all of us out here to help him. One phone call and we all stopped our lives and jumped on a plane."

"I'm sorry, I shouldn't have—"

"Wasn't about you. It was about him. Who he is to us."

The unsaid accusation is that Tyler doesn't mean as much to me as he does to them. And he's not wrong. I've been pushing Tyler away until last night. Was it really only hours ago that we...made love? Fucked? I don't even know what to call it. Giving in?

"You're making everyone nuts. We came here to help you because Tyler asked. And you don't have the common courtesy to sit your ass in a chair and stay there when we're getting terrible news about Blake. He's family."

The implication is that I'm not. It doesn't need to be said because it's true.

"Then I go round you up so Tyler doesn't lose his fucking mind, and you hide in the bathroom?" He somehow gets bigger in his anger with me. "The team has enough on their plate without you disappearing every other minute. Their missions doubled overnight. They still need to find the bastard who did this to Blake and put him down in whatever form that takes. That works out well for you. Right?"

I nod.

"But more importantly, they have to support Blake. Anything he needs, all the support, one hundred percent.

Because no matter what the docs think or tell us, that man is going to live."

"How can you know that?" I regret blurting that out the second it leaves my lips.

Stone's eyes narrow. "It's not his time to go. If he was ready, he wouldn't have survived the wreck. Wouldn't have miraculously been able to reach his phone and call his team back. The energy of his family surrounds him right now. Carrying the load for him in their souls. As his family, we're going to anchor him here and be with him every second as he goes through whatever hell his recovery is going to require. You know why?"

I shake my head. Aside from Tyler, I've never had people who cared about me that deeply. My parents were older and otherwise occupied with their careers. I was probably a whim or a mistake. They passed before I could ask. Not that I would have.

"Because Tyler's one of the good guys. You don't give up on the good guys. And you don't give up on family. Not if that's who you truly are."

I hear what Stone isn't saying. I'm not Tyler's family. Despite our marriage, we're not really together. Every time he focuses on me—what I need—he loses something. His job. His friend. It's up to me to stop putting him in the position of choosing. Instead, I have to make the right choice. It's obvious what I have to do, but I'm dreading it. Breaking it off with Tyler is harder than ripping out my own guts. But if I selfishly stay with him—if he keeps coming to my rescue—what will it cost him next?

I can't be responsible for another disaster. "I understand."

Stone relaxes back in the driver's seat as the sun finishes its trek above the horizon. The sky is vivid shades of pink, orange, and red before resuming the beautiful blue the state is known for. I should find it hopeful, but I'm more inclined to believe the sailors' warning associated with red skies in the morning. A storm is coming.

Stone drives us back to the rounded brick buildings where his team waits to hear about their brother. I follow him back to the ER. Eliot and Cade remain huddled in the same spot. Alex is stretched out, ankles crossed, and snoring softly. Tyler isn't there. Stone ignores me and sits next to Eliot, who shakes his head at whatever Stone asks him.

I sit near Alex, by myself but visible, before fishing my phone out of my purse.

Me: *I need help.*

Katherine: *What's going on?*

Me: *There was an accident. Blake was badly injured. We all came to Colorado Springs, but I'm in the way. Distracting the guys when they need to focus on Blake. And I don't want to make any phone calls and upset them. I was hoping you could help me get back to Alabaster?*

Katherine: *Of course. I'll make the calls. Can you get to the airport?*

Me: *I can get a rideshare, no problem.*

She taps back with a thumbs-up. I stare at the screen for a few minutes before relaxing my arm and letting my cell rest on my leg. I'll feel the vibration when she texts back. For now, I'll sit back and wait and stay in plain sight so I don't piss anyone off again.

I must doze off because the rumble of the phone jolts me awake. I quickly check my messages.

Katherine: *You're booked on a private flight, tentatively taking off in three hours. Go to the private hangar. The pilot will be waiting for you. Gabe'll pick you up in Aspen. You'll stay with us.*

Me: *Thank you. I'll pay you back.*

Katherine: *Don't worry about it for a minute. I'm glad I can help. You've done so much for Gabe and me. Consider this a thank you.*

Me: *I appreciate it. But I can't stay with you. It would put you at risk.*

Katherine: *This is Gabe. You're staying with us. Don't worry, I know how to play security. We can keep you safe until this asshole is caught. In fact, I have news for Tyler. Is he there?*

Me: *Not at the moment.*

Katherine: *Betty's gone missing. Local, county, and state cops are looking for the man staying at her place. From STL. Betty's phone was found in her place, along with a lot of blood.*

Me: *Maybe you should call Tyler with that.*

Because if I tell Tyler about crushed phones and blood, there is no way I'll be getting on the plane.

Katherine sends the pilot's name, the hangar directions, and the plane tail number just for security. I have my driver's license so I can prove who I am.

I look up directions from the hospital to the airport and get an idea of what a ride share will cost me. Damn. This is not a short ride. There's a bus, but Tyler would shit himself if I got on a public bus. I search for a shuttle service and scroll through the results when a shadow crosses the screen.

Tyler stands right behind me. "Going somewhere?"

TWENTY-ONE

Tyler

I CLIMB BACK into Amy's car and set a timer for forty-five minutes on my phone—the flight time between Colorado Springs and Aspen. Gabe will pick her up there. As the private jet lifts off and flies directly over my head, I start the timer and ignore the fact my heart is on the plane with her. I ache with the emptiness. The urgency to get her back in my arms, back in bed, get back inside her, compels me to drive straight to Alabaster and then take her somewhere we'll never be found. But I can't leave my team. And I shouldn't let Amy leave.

Our argument rings in my ears. "I'm in the way, a distraction when you need to focus on your team," she said. I disagreed, though she wasn't wrong. But it's temporary. I'll get back to Alabaster as soon as Blake is stabilized and Eliot and Cade have what they need. It sounds logical, but my heart tells me I'm a bastard for letting her out of my sight.

I grip the steering wheel until my knuckles turn white. My

emotions are ruling my head. I have to be logical. Gabe and Katherine are perfectly capable of keeping Amy safe. No one will know she's at their remote lodge. Gabe has military training. I could keep listing all the reasons I shouldn't worry, but it won't change a thing. I call Gabe. "She's on the way."

"I'm walking to the truck now. The drive to Aspen and the flight time are nearly the same. Katherine made arrangements for me to meet the pilot on the tarmac and escort Amy personally."

"You carrying?"

"Of course. I'll take care of her as if she was mine. No worries, brother."

"Katherine's not going with you?"

"We've just got another foster trio. Six, nine, and twelve. She's staying with them."

I have so much respect for Gabe and his wife taking on the kids who have no one else. An image of Amy rounded with my child flashes like a photograph before my eyes. We're on the edge of the fertility age limits, but it's possible. I can see it so clearly—as if it was already true. A little girl with Amy's sweet brown eyes, inspecting presents under a Christmas tree. Stockings hanging on a mantel. Midnight in our bedroom, playing naughty elf games and trying to be quiet. Fuck. I want that to be real. It knocks the breath out of me.

Gabe is saying something. I try to focus. "...still searching but haven't found her yet."

"Who?"

"Betty. The innkeeper."

"Right." The woman is probably dead. "Just make sure Amy isn't alone for a second."

"No one is getting their hands on my friend. Amy means the world to Katherine. I don't disappoint my wife. Ever."

I would love to be able to say the same thing. I'm working

on it. One problem at a time. "I'll have my phone on. Call me as soon as you have her."

Gabe makes me another promise I half hear because while I'm desperate to keep Amy safe, I'm completely distracted by thoughts of our future and the situation with Blake. I'm halfway back to the hospital when my phone alarm buzzes. She should have landed. I keep driving, controlling my panic with every passing second. When the phone rings, I put it on speaker. "Got your girl."

"I'm a woman, Gabe." Amy's voice comes through loud and clear.

"You're safe?"

"I'm fine," she answers. "An hour on a private jet is no hardship."

I'd love to have her get used to that, but I'm a retired guy on a fixed income now. I'll spoil her in other ways. But I can't think about that right now. "Call me when you get home."

"Will do, boss," Gabe replies before ending the call.

Back at the hospital, Blake has been moved from recovery to ICU. Alex leads me from the ER waiting room to the new floor. The rest of the team is seated in an echo of a faux airport lounge from downstairs. I don't know if I like this hospital's modern, everything-is-fine feel. The exhausted faces of fearful family members don't match the vibe the decorator went for. We cross to the back corner where the guys huddle.

Eliot and Cade were already in to see Blake for a short visit. There's a grim look in Eliot's eye, but his report has a hopeful tone. Likely, he's trying to keep it together for Cade.

"This is going to be a long road." I don't want to keep saying that, but it has to sink in eventually. "I know you guys want to live here twenty-four seven, but the reality is, they'll be checking you into a room to recover if you try."

"We aren't leaving him alone." Cade crosses his arms, I

assume to keep from punching me, and I'm grateful. I'm barely holding on as well.

"I was going to suggest we rent a hotel room, or maybe a small house on a month-to-month. You can stagger your coverage." Sleep and showers will go a long way toward sustaining their vigil.

"Any word on Brambilla?" Eliot asks.

"Multiple agencies looking for him. Aside from the attack on Blake, I'm pretty certain he ended the woman who owns the place where he's been staying. But I have serious doubts about them finding him." I meet Eliot's gaze. "To be honest, I hate Amy being anywhere near that town without me."

"I'm sorry we can't continue to help with her protection." Eliot turns to Cade. "Blake needs everything we can give him right now."

"Don't apologize," I say. "I want to support you, but I have to find this fucker. For Amy and for Blake."

Stone places his hand on Cade's shoulder. "The house is a good idea."

Cade nods, his entire body slumping under the acceptance that Blake isn't walking out of the hospital anytime soon.

"Let me take care of that," I say.

"I need to make a few phone calls, too." Stone pulls his cell out of his pocket. "We're staying until the next visitation window. I want Blake to know all of us are focused on him. But then we have to go put that sick fuck down. Eliminate the threat so we can focus on our boy."

The team nods in agreement. I leave Alex with Eliot and Cade as I search for anything rentable close to the hospital. Stone wanders away in the opposite direction.

Before I find a place, the nurse announces that we can do a ten-minute visit. Two of us only. Stone and I head for the door.

"I called Pierce, the bouncer from the club," Stone says as

we follow the nurse. "I want our guys protected, and he can do the running around. Make sure they eat. Drive them back and forth to the house. All the shit we can't do until we finish with Brambilla."

"Good call." I'm impressed Stone thought of that. "You had his number?"

"Put a call into the club. He happened to answer. Saved me some begging."

I couldn't imagine Stone begging for anything. But I guess when he has to ask for anything instead of command it, it feels like begging to him. If we weren't walking back to see Blake, I might even laugh at the thought.

We step behind the curtain that functions as a door, and I freeze. I was prepared for the mess of tubes and wires, and the stands of beeping electronic boxes. The mess on the bed that is what's left of my friend kicks me hard in the gut. Blake's eyes are black, his swollen face is scraped up, and a tube in his mouth pumps air into his lungs. Thankfully, there doesn't seem to be a head injury, maybe because the airbags did their job and kept him alive. He doesn't even have a gown, just a blanket pulled up to his waist, covering the casts on both his legs. There's a gauze patch taped on the side of his abdomen, a clean spot among the darkening bruises. Probably where they cut him open to remove his spleen. The coffee I drank down a few hours earlier rises with bile in my throat. Stone makes a grunting sound. I'm not the only one impacted by our friend's appearance.

I force myself to close the distance to the bed and carefully place my hand on Blake's bare shoulder. "We're here for you, Blake. All of us. Just hang in there, buddy. The docs will fix you up, and the guys will be with you. You're not alone." Please, God. Don't take him. We need him here. I swallow back the tears that are building.

Stone brushes his fingers through Blake's hair. "You will get better. There is nothing you can't endure to live. Your boys need you. So, you focus on healing. Hear me?"

If Blake could be healed by sheer willpower, he'd already be better because a tremendous amount of energy is flowing from all the guys in his direction. His family. Blake doesn't have anyone else but them. And we will never be the same if he doesn't make it.

The nurse pulls back the curtain and looks at me pointedly. For a short guy, he has a very strong personality. I don't even think about arguing. Stone pauses as we pass. "Take care of him."

"Anything and everything I can," the guy answers. His quietly confident promise somehow helps me walk out when it's the last thing I want to do.

Stone nods, and we march back to the waiting room. I leave part of my soul by that bed. The part Blake will take with him if he doesn't make it.

My phone rings, and Alex hands it to me. It's the owner of the house calling to confirm we can rent it for a month. It's not cheap, but I don't care. I can cover the first month and we can figure out what to do next in a few weeks. "Got you a three-bedroom," I tell Eliot and Cade.

"We don't need that much space," Cade argues.

"You do," Stone responds for me. "Because Pierce Jaramillo is going to be living with you, and when Reed finishes his body-guard job, you know he's coming out here. Might come sooner."

"Pierce from the club?" Eliot asks.

"Yes."

"Why?" Cade's face wrinkles with confusion.

"I asked him to. I'm paying him to watch over you two."

"We can't afford that." Eliot sounds so beat down.

"I'm paying," Stone repeats. "And I'm covering your

incomes until you can book jobs again. Right now, Blake is your biggest and most important job." His tone brooks no argument.

"And Reed will take care of any business or personal issues that have to be handled back home," I add.

"He said as much when I called him after seeing Blake in the ICU," Eliot says.

"Your only focus is Blake." Stone crosses his arms and widens his stance. He uses that same pose with bratty subs or fuckup Doms. There is no arguing.

I glance at my watch. "I need to get on the road."

"I'm going with Tyler. Sooner we put this son of a bitch down, the better," Stone says.

"Me, too," Alex says as he steps closer to me. "First, I want to see if I can get that nurse to give me five minutes with Blake."

"Good luck. He seems like a stickler." Which overall makes me very happy. I need someone who is on top of the details taking care of Blake.

"Southern charm can overcome stickler," Alex drawls as he saunters over to the desk. Sure enough. He flashes a thumbs-up before he disappears behind the locked door.

"Do you two need anything before we go?" I feel guilty about leaving. Guilty about not leaving sooner. But once Brambilla is handled, I can give Eliot and Cade the support they need with one hundred percent focus.

Twenty minutes later, the three of us pile into Amy's car. Alex sits in the back, hoping to sleep. As soon as I'm on the highway, Stone shifts in the passenger seat. "This situation with Blake isn't your fault."

"I know. Logically."

"You two are too much alike."

"Who?" I ask.

"Amy." Stone flicks the air vent away from him. "Both of you feel responsible for what that criminal did. Her thinking's even more twisted. She doesn't believe she deserves protection."

"Of course she does."

"And you don't believe you deserve to have her."

Stone's words hit me like a bat to the skull, but he's not wrong. I shake my head—not disagreeing, but to get my brain working again.

"When are you going to admit to yourself that you've been gone over this woman since the first time your hand connected with her backside?"

"Before that. From the moment I saw her." I don't have any lies left, not even for myself.

"If you don't make this right, quick, you'll never get the chance again. Ask me how I know."

It's not really an invitation. I've always known Stone had a story about the one who got away. The wisdom he gained too late.

"After we get this guy and Blake is released from the hospital, what will the team do? Will Blake rehab here or in St. Louis?" I glance at him. "Because I'll be honest, I don't want to lose my brothers who've kept me sane all these years. I don't want to choose between the love of my life and my family. Does that make me selfish?" Asking for everything is a bit much. "It's just I don't think Amy will go back. She shouldn't."

Stone grunts. "About that—"

TWENTY-TWO

Amy

I PUT another slice of pepperoni pizza on my paper plate and return to the living room where Katherine, Gabe, and their three foster kids are deep into Gabe's favorite movie. I can't focus on the fantasy plot, not when Blake might die and Tyler is torn between taking care of me and his loyalty to his team. He should never have come here. As Stone reminded me, I'm not his family. And as wonderful as Katherine and Gabe are, I'm not their family either. I don't belong here any more than I belonged at the hospital.

As soon as the movie ends, Katherine organizes the cleanup and prep for bed. The kids are adorable but kind of lost. Rudderless. And I can completely relate, but I'm too old to depend on someone to guide me through the daily chores of life like brushing my teeth and putting on my pajamas. Maybe there should be adult foster care for when life gets too overwhelming. Someone to call in and hand over the issues

I'm facing. Someone who can remind me to take care of myself. Maybe I treated Tyler like he was that person. I had no right to ask that of him, to involve his team. He's my husband on paper, but would my husband want me to be this needy?

"I should go," I tell Gabe as soon as the kids are upstairs. "If you could give me a ride back to the Sunflower, I can take care of myself."

"No." Gabe's single-word response is like a slap.

"What?" Gabe is never that blunt.

"Not only no but hell no. You're safe here. Betty's still missing, and there are teams of law enforcement searching for who I suspect is the guy after you. I send you back to the Sunflower alone, and Tyler won't just be spanking *your* ass. He'll be kicking mine."

Flames burn my cheeks. How could Tyler have outed me to my friends? "I don't know what you're talking about."

"Amy, I'm not trying to embarrass you. Just get your attention. You're safe here. The attic suite's ready for you."

"What did Tyler tell you?"

"Nothing specifically. I just overheard a conversation. Plus, the way he interacts with you." Gabe shrugs. "I lived with other guys for years in the military. Not much I haven't seen or heard. Everyone has their own tick, the thing that winds their clock. No judgment."

I nod, but the heat still burns my face. Up until a few weeks ago, my entire life, even my name, was private—a secret I held close to my chest. If I could sink into a hole right now, that would be ideal.

"But you can't go running off. People care about you, a lot of people. Katherine cares about you. You know I do. If it were up to me, you would stay with us forever, you know that. You're family."

My breath catches. I'm not family, but he's treating me like I am. Tyler said almost the same thing.

Katherine appears on the stairs. "Wine?"

I nod.

Gabe gives me a brief one-arm embrace before heading to the kitchen. He opens a bottle for us. "I'm going to hit the sack. I'll take breakfast duty with the kids."

Katherine steps into his embrace and runs her fingers through his thick, dark hair. "I'll wake you up when I come in."

I'm pretty sure I wasn't supposed to overhear that, but the sexy promise makes me miss Tyler even more. I turn away from their kiss and pour two glasses.

"Night, Amy. See you in the morning." Gabe's already walking to their bedroom beyond the stairs.

Katherine picks up her wine and hands me the other one. "Let's sit in the living room so we can be comfortable."

I snatch the bottle and follow her, settling on one end of their couch.

"Gabe said the missing gangster might have killed Betty."

I shiver. Betty is a nightmare, but no one deserves to be on the wrong end of Enzo's violent streak. "He's a very violent man. I know this from when I dated him. Briefly."

"You dated the guy trying to kill you? Is that the real reason you were in protection?"

"No. Well, not really. Maybe subconsciously, I turned in the family for falsifying tax records to get out of my situation. Enzo Junior was adamant about keeping me, but he was abusive. We'd only dated a couple of months before I broke it off. His father backed me up—made it clear I was not to be harmed—because he liked having me as his accountant. Even sent Junior out of the country. In hindsight, that might have been what tipped me off to look closer."

"What do you mean abusive?"

I take a sip of my wine. Am I really going to explain my kink and the risk it poses to my friend? Having tasted it at the club with Tyler, I don't want to lock out that side of myself again. But if Gabe knows, so does Katherine. I might as well come clean. "Have you ever heard of BDSM?"

"I lived in New York, and after that shady trilogy of books came out and hit the end aisle display at the bookstore, the secret was out."

"Well, I like some kink in my sex life." I bite my lip, unable to meet her eyes as I wait for her response.

"Still doesn't explain your relationship with Junior."

Warmth that isn't due to the wine slides through my heart, and my muscles relax. She isn't judging me. "He took it too far. Didn't respect my boundaries. He...um...he basically raped me before we broke up."

Katherine sets her wine down, crosses to me, and wraps me in a hug. "That fucking bastard."

"Yeah, he was." I've never said it out loud. I couldn't go to the police when it happened. It was too much to explain, and if I had turned his son in to the cops, Enzo Sr. would have made me disappear before the paperwork on the investigation was even started. Admitting what he did to someone else makes my experience more real, not just a figment of my memory or imagination. The echo of my assault—physical, emotional, mental— blankets me, and I'm in the past for a moment. It still stings and shames me, but not so intensely. He was responsible for violating me. Nothing I did or didn't do was *asking* for rape. I sniff back the building tears. "If I could go back and, change anything to avoid that night, I would in a heartbeat."

Katherine leans back and looks into my eyes. "It wasn't your fault. Using your preferences against you, hurting you beyond your limits, and taking actions too far are inexcusable. Did you get counseling after?"

"I probably should have, but it didn't feel safe to tell anyone in St. Louis."

"You could see someone now." Katherine grabs a box of tissues and hands them to me. I didn't realize I was crying.

"I might. After Tyler—" A sob breaks free at the thought of him leaving without me.

"How long have you known him? Does he know about your preferences? About what happened?"

"I never told him what happened. Not specifically. He might suspect."

Katherine narrows her eyes. "He's more than your handler."

"I met him at a club in St. Louis. I started going after I broke things off with Enzo. I was so stressed, and I had to have a release. Get out of my head but in a public place. Somewhere safe."

"You were seeing Tyler before all this happened?"

"Not exactly. It took me a few months to figure out what the Brambilla family was up to and how they were laundering their money." I twist the wineglass in my hand. Even thinking about the Brambillas makes me edgy. "I had to be super careful to hide my investigation. I went to the club to relieve my anxiety. There's something that happens when I...I get what I need. I can completely sink into the experience and let everything else go."

"Like meditating?"

"Probably? I've never meditated."

"Tyler was giving you what you need?" Katherine's voice is accepting, approving even.

"Yes, but we never...uh...we never had sex."

"Huh?"

"I couldn't. Well, at least not for a long time. It took me a while to trust him at all even though I was attracted to him the moment I saw him. I went to the club for months before we had any...interaction." My cheeks heat.

"But you have now. You've had sex with him." Her soft voice coaxes the truth from me.

I nod and stare into my half-empty glass.

"Was it worth waiting for?"

It was, but I can't admit that out loud. It will make losing him hurt even more. "It was an old dream. Our lives are very different now. I live here. He lives in St. Louis. Everything about us is fake."

Katherine smiles. "Gabe and I faked being married before we ever really got together."

"What?"

"You remember. The lodgers we weren't supposed to have?"

I do. "But it's different. You chose to leave your old life because you found the man of your dreams."

"You didn't have to actually marry Tyler when you went into the program. Especially since you already had a relationship of sorts. You could have requested a different agent be assigned to your case. Legitimately so. But you didn't."

"True." I put my glass on the table. The wine and pizza churn in my gut with the honesty Katherine pushes. "A part of me was terrified of being truly alone. Even though we never had actual sex, I trusted him. And all this time out here has been easier to deal with, knowing he was tied to me. Knowing he would come to visit or I could call him. Being married was like a safety cocoon wrapped around me. I didn't have to date or deal with men at all."

"Enzo really messed you up."

He had. And I kept Tyler at an emotional distance while using him. "But then I watched you and Gabe find love..." I twist my wedding ring out of habit. "But I'm so tired of being alone. I wanted Tyler to come to my rescue. I'm pretty sure that's why I broke the rule about having nothing to do with finances or taxes or bookkeeping."

"Taking the treasurer role with ABBA."

"The closer you got to your wedding date, the more alone I felt." I wrap my arms around my roiling gut. I can't believe I'm confessing all of this. But I'm losing Tyler. Katherine is my friend. I have to be honest with someone. "It's like I knew that breaking the rules would make him come out here. I totally manipulated him and jacked everything up." I drop my gaze to the soft leather couch. I can't face her.

Katherine scoffs. "You can't take responsibility for someone else's sins. You didn't attack Blake. You didn't make Betty disappear. And you didn't ask Tyler to quit his job. He could have notified you, sent divorce paperwork, and walked away. Those were choices other people made." She puts her hand on my knee. The warmth seeps into my jeans, working its way deeper. "Seems like you have a choice to make too. Are you going to let Tyler return to St. Louis without you? Or are you going to ask to go with him? Or, even better, ask him to stay?"

My heart aches. I do have a choice to make.

Katherine picks up our glasses and the bottle. "I'll leave you to think about it."

As soon as she closes her bedroom door, I drag myself up the two flights of stairs as quietly as I can, and each step leads me to a firm decision. There is only one real choice because I love him. For better or worse, until I die. The moment I admit it, my doubts whisk away. I've loved him for a long time and never let myself acknowledge it. I won't bury my feelings any longer. If Tyler still wants me, I'll be with him no matter where we live. I'm keeping my husband.

TWENTY-THREE

Tyler

RAIN IS POURING DOWN. I keep my eyes on the road despite the urge to check if it's really Stone sitting next to me.

"You want to open a club?" I did not have Stone deciding to open a new BDSM club on my bingo card. To be fair, I didn't have Blake being run off the road and nearly killed either.

"Think about it. The club in Colorado Springs is packed. There's demand. We'll do something more high-end. Make it exclusive with a good cover story. And private rooms so it's not just a dungeon."

"Cover story?" More like fantasy fiction.

"The Aspen airport is packed with jets no matter the season."

"True."

"Tourists fill up all these little towns, even if they aren't jet-setters. They're coming here to celebrate and have an experience. Spend their money lavishly, based on the price of baked goods."

Stone has lost his marbles. I should turn around and drive back to the hospital so he can get his head examined. "What do baked goods have to do with a BDSM club?"

"If someone's willing to spend three hundred or more on a birthday cake in this area, and that's what private bakers are charging, what do you think they'd pay for a week or month or yearlong membership to a private club? Topside will be a restaurant, classic, talented chefs—you know."

"Country club vibe." I nod, an image of his plan starting to form. But it's like an adult version of a theme park, all fantasy and not even close to reality. Reality involves mortgages, property taxes, and certificates of occupancy.

"Down below, a members-only area. A private dungeon with play rooms. If we find the right property, we could even have some condos to rent."

"You want to open a BDSM resort in the mountains of Colorado."

"If I can find the right property."

"Why now and why here? Don't we have enough to deal with?" Like a killer after my wife or our brother who might die. And Stone is playing let's pretend?

"Had the idea as soon as we hit Pandora's. And it solves a ton of problems."

No, it creates a hundred more. "Name one."

"We can all stay here and have jobs and an income. Alex can oversee the construction. Eliot's team can design the network and security. I can bankroll the effort and manage the dungeon. Amy's a wiz with vacation rentals and design. And you're a details guy. The man with a plan, always. You can be the general manager and handle the day-to-day operations.

Hell, you've probably thought of several things I'm ignoring already."

The wet road is particularly twisty, allowing me to be quiet and consider what Stone's saying. A private resort club actually has potential. "You already have this all figured out. Where's the property?"

"Between Alabaster and Aspen. I haven't put in an offer yet. I wasn't sure we had all agreed to stay."

"Did we agree?" I'm staying, but I'm only one person. I have no idea what Amy will think about this.

"Everyone has loved being out here. No one bellyached about going back. Blake is in for a long recovery. Months to years. That hospital is well-funded and well-staffed. Wasn't a goddamn knife and gun club running through there."

Stone raises a valid point. St. Louis has become more and more dangerous in the past few years. A lot of talented people are leaving.

"Eliot asked Pierce about security gigs in the area. With all the money floating around this place, contracts must open up all the time."

Stone's not wrong. I check the rearview. Alex is awake and staring straight ahead. "What about you, Alex?"

Alex lifts a shoulder. I focus back on the road.

"As long as I ain't in the state of Texas, dude, it don't matter where I am. It's all good."

I looked into Alex's background, but the details of why he had to avoid his home state were elusive.

"Gabe mentioned needing help with some construction jobs," Alex adds.

Stone clears his throat. "If we do this, you'll be busy with *our* project. Gabe too, most likely."

How much money did Stone have stashed back? "How will

the investment work?" I can sell my house in Kirkwood. "I'd want to buy in. Be a partner."

"Of course you do." Stone huffs. "I don't have it all figured out, but that won't be a problem."

We keep hashing out details, tossing out ideas but rejecting most of them. Planning a future is a nice distraction from the shit reality we still have to deal with. When we pull up to the Ponderosa, I check my watch. Too early. I park next to Gabe's truck in his pea gravel parking area. "I'm going to see if anyone's up. Coming in?"

"We'll wait here." Stone crosses his arms and closes his eyes. We could all use some sleep, but I need Amy with me.

I check the front door. Locked. Good. Cringing at the disruption I'm causing, I knock lightly. Only a few moments pass before a small force vibrates the door. Gabe's voice reaches beyond the wood panel, "Don't open that door. Go back in the kitchen and eat your breakfast."

The lock clicks back, and an inch of Gabe's face appears. He steps back, swings the door wide, and smiles when he recognizes me, holstering his pistol in a smooth, subtle move. Can't even tell he's armed after he pulls his shirt back down. "Amy's upstairs taking a shower."

A longing to join her flashes through me. "You're up early."

"These munchkins don't appreciate the joys of sleeping in." Three kiddos occupy seats at the dining table. "I promised we could go into town and find Halloween decorations."

"Bit early?"

"Tell the stores that. I think they'd put out the sh...stuff on the fifth of July if they could get away with it."

I smile at Gabe's joke, accept a cup of coffee, and try not to pace while glancing at the stairs every thirty seconds. Finally, Amy descends, reminding me why I broke every rule to marry her. She's beautiful—fresh, bare face with her hair in a ponytail. Her smile lands with a blow to my heart. God, I love this woman.

"You're here?" She reaches the bottom but stops just out of reach. "Thought you'd still be at the hospital." She gasps, her hand going to her mouth, eyes wide and watery. "Blake didn't—"

I tug her to me. "He's alive. Nothing's changed."

"Thank goodness." She squirms out of my hold. "Can I go home? Being here with Katherine, Gabe, and the kids has been wonderful, but I have so much I could be doing. Does that sound horrible?"

"I understand." It's rough when the immediate problem can't be fixed, feeling useless or worse powerless in a crisis. "Stone and Alex are in the car."

"Tell them to come in. I mean..." She glances to the kitchen where Gabe refills plates with scrambled eggs and buttered toast. The toast is well done, but the kids don't complain. "I'm sure Gabe would like to see them."

"The guys are ready to sleep in a bed. Take a shower."

"Let me say goodbye then."

I take her hand in mine, her fingers cold. We move toward the insta-family.

Adoption could work.

Where did *that* come from? One thing at a time. "Gabe, any updates on the..."

"Hunt?" He fills in.

"Yeah."

"No sign. But they have enough to keep the beast in a cage for a very long time." Gabe's using coded language because of the kids, but it seems the law has found at least one body.

"We're headed back to the Sunflower."

"Thank you for everything," Amy blurts, cutting off my own words of gratitude. "Tell Katherine I'll call her?"

Gabe gives a brief nod. "You need anything..."

"I know." Amy frees herself from my grip to give Gabe a quick hug.

He pats her back twice and releases her. "Be safe."

TWENTY-FOUR

Amy

TYLER TAKES command as soon as we park under the carport at the Sunflower. "Alex, stay in the car with Amy while Stone and I check the perimeter."

The rain has paused, but the overcast sky keeps everything in shadows. The wind is whipping up, causing the tree branches to sway. The guys divide up and disappear around the back of the house. A few minutes later, Stone and Tyler reappear and move to the front door. There should be nothing to worry about inside—the alarms have been quiet. They unlock the door and push it open, standing to either side. When nothing happens, not surprisingly, they head in with handguns leading the way. Several minutes go by before they come out. I refrain from rolling my eyes. This is such overkill. The last place Enzo will be is where they expect him. He'd have to be a complete moron to show up here.

Tyler comes out alone, the gun probably tucked away on

his body somewhere since he's no longer holding it. The rain picks up again, pouring down stronger than before. He opens my car door. "All clear."

He and Alex flank me as we run to the front door. I feel like a playactor in an action film. This is ridiculous. Once inside, Tyler locks the door behind us.

A strange thumping sound booms from the back of the house, and I startle. Maybe they aren't overreacting. Maybe I'm in denial. "Do you hear that?"

"Didn't when I went out back. I'll check it again. Let me grab a rain jacket."

"I'll come with," Alex says.

I pull my wet shirt away from my chest. I've been wearing these clothes for what seems like days. "I need to get changed."

"Stone's taking a shower," Tyler says from the stairwell. "Stay inside."

"I'll be in the basement." I head straight for the kitchen. Tea is the only solution to this crazy anxiety. Tyler's right to be so careful, but I struggle to believe I'm in danger when I'm safe at home. I don't *want* to believe it. I plug in the kettle and flip it on before I drop my purse in the office. After navigating the narrow wooden stairway, I tug my shirt over my head and drop it in the washer. A long-sleeved knit waits for me in a pile of folded clothes I hadn't had time to put away yet. The clean, dry warmth is like a hug. Dragging off my soaked jeans takes a little longer. My fuzzy pajama bottoms offer welcome relief from the cold, damp denim. All I need now is a cup of tea.

"Oh!" I'm surprised Tyler is in the kitchen. "Did you figure out the noise?"

"Gutter. Alex pulled the broken piece down so it didn't beat up the siding. He's taking a shower and changing, then we'll head to the store. Stone will be here."

I sniff. "You should change too."

Tyler tucks his nose to his armpit. "Do I stink?"

"Probably. But don't you want a shower? Some clean clothes?" *Why am I trying to delay his leaving?*

"Later." He chuckles. "Right this second, I need a bathroom break. It was a long drive."

I shake my head. "You don't need my permission."

"Had to make sure you were okay first." Those words warm me more than my comfy clothes.

"Go." I shoo him away. "I'll be right here, making tea. Nothing to worry about."

He turns and jogs away. They better catch Enzo quickly. I can't live with all this tension. Poking through my tea boxes, I find my favorite herbal blend. I grab a mug from the cabinet above the kettle, and a gust of cold air blasts through the kitchen. I freeze, expecting...

I don't know what. Tyler's paranoia is catching.

I put down the cup and move to the front door.

No.

My heart slams up my throat, choking off my air.

He's here.

Icy terror rushes through my veins.

Enzo locks onto me the second I move. His face is a horrifying mask of hatred. He has on mud-caked shoes and a grime-streaked shirt, and he holds a gun at the end of one sleeve. "You fucking cunt."

His quiet tone is a cold blade up my back. My heart pounds so hard I'm going to break a rib.

I dart back into the kitchen. Nowhere to go. No second exit—only the basement or my small closet office. It has a lock. I move, but Enzo's fingers dig into my shoulder, hitting a pressure point. My knees weaken from the pain.

"Payback time."

"For what?" I blurt, searching desperately for a weapon. I should scream, but the guys are upstairs. They won't hear me.

He wrenches me around to face him. My back slams into the counter. I whimper, and he grins. "You killed my father. I'm gonna fuck you half dead before I put a bullet in your skull. You—"

I snatch the kettle and bash him in the head with it as hard as I can. Boiling water cascades over his face. He screams and lifts the gun. The hole on the barrel is huge, blocking out the entire kitchen.

I brace for the blast that will rip out my heart.

Enzo's arm juts up. The boom of the gun firing deafens me.

Tyler has Enzo in a chokehold with one arm, the other gripping Enzo's elbow. The bullet meant for me is embedded in the ceiling. A huge hole that would have killed me. I back up, getting out of Tyler's way. Please don't let him get hurt.

Tyler smacks Enzo's wrist on the counter. Enzo screams, and the gun clangs to the floor. But he's still fighting, wrenching his body against Tyler's hold. If Enzo gets free...

Please don't let anything happen to Tyler, I pray.

With a leg sweep, Enzo drops. The psycho has shifted from screaming in pain to a stream of incoherent obscenities. Tyler wrenches Enzo's arm up behind. "Shut the hell up, you piece of shit."

"I'll kill you and that—"

Tyler grabs Enzo's hair and smacks his face into the tile floor. "I'm too well trained to kill you without cause. But I will fuck you up if you say one more word." Tyler pulls his weapon from behind his back and points it at Enzo's head. "Call the police."

Tyler's command gets me moving. I dart into the office and nearly lock the door. But if Enzo moves a hair, he'll be the one taking a bullet.

I explain the situation to the emergency operator who answers my cell call. Adrenaline hits my system hard, and I lean against the doorframe. Shakes engulf me. This is insane.

I nearly died.

I should have died.

How did Tyler get to the kitchen without me seeing him? All I could see was Enzo's gun. All I could hear was his hateful voice. All I want is for Tyler to hold me until I stop quaking, but he has his hands full. I slide down to a crouch and keep responding to the operator who tells me the police are nearly here. At least Enzo is quiet. Both of us know Tyler wasn't kidding when he told Enzo to shut up.

"Drop the weapon," an unfamiliar deep voice barks the command. A police officer appears, barrel first, in my kitchen door. He's pointing his gun at Tyler.

What the hell? I stand.

"Ma'am, stay where you are."

Freezing, I raise my hands to my chest palms out. The emergency operator's voice echos from my cell phone.

Stone and Alex are at the far end with a second officer.

"Tyler Davis. FBI. Going to set this down right here." Tyler places his gun on the countertop and lifts his hands. His knee is still firmly planted on Enzo's back.

"Arrest this man. He assaulted me. Broke my wrist. And that bitch attacked me," Enzo wheezes from the floor, but nobody pays him any attention. The police have been looking for him. He can't play the victim.

"We'll take it from here." The officer is much calmer now that he's the only one with a weapon in hand. He picks up Enzo's gun and places it next to Tyler's.

Tyler rises off Enzo, using the dirtbag as a push point. The officer handcuffs Enzo and turns him over. Ouch.

"Call an ambulance," the cop instructs his partner.

Enzo's face is blistered. One eye is closed, the eyelid too puffy to open. A part of me is sick that I did that, and the other part is kind of proud that I tried to defend myself.

The cops march Enzo out of my house telling him he's under arrest for the murder of Betty Keppel and another man's name I don't recognize. "And the attempted murder of Blake Foster."

My name could have been on that list. The room spins. Before I hit the floor, Tyler wraps his body around me, holding me together. He guides me into the living room.

We take turns giving statements. The barrel of the gun and Tyler wrestling with Enzo flashes like scenes of a movie behind my eyes. Tyler calls Gabe to tell him what happened. Stone—his face a stern mask—paces through the downstairs, checking each door and window to ensure everything is locked. One thing doesn't make sense.

"How did Enzo get in without breaking down the door?" I ask Tyler once he's done talking to Gabe.

Tyler looks pointedly at Alex.

Alex raises his hands and shakes his head. "I don't have the keys to this place. You let us out."

Tyler's gaze bounces from Alex, to the door, to the kitchen and lands on me. "I let you down. I'm so sorry."

I reach for him, and he takes my hand. "No. You saved me. Again."

Tyler settles on the couch. "I'll always save you. If you'll let me."

My shoulders slump. That would only be possible if he were staying.

Alex asks for the keys to my car so he can go to the hardware store for the piece of gutter.

"Don't forget the bullet hole in the kitchen," I say. "I don't want to explain that to our guests." A bullet hole in my B and B.

Tears slide down my face. It's completely irrational. I'm safe, so why am I crying now?

Tyler scoots closer to where I'm sitting on the couch and strokes my arm. "It's okay. It's all over."

"Is it? Blake's still in the hospital. I'm back to being a witness to a crime for a mob boss. It's not over. If anything, I'm right back in hell."

Tyler takes my chin, so I'm looking directly at him. "You won't have to testify. You didn't see him murder anyone. You didn't see him push Blake off the road."

Another wave of sadness hits me. I hate Enzo. Despite my resistance to hating anyone, I truly hate the man for bringing nothing but pain and grief into my life. My friends' lives. Part of me can't believe he won't continue to terrorize me in the future.

"What about his..." I wave my hand in the air, looking for the right word. "Family." Although that seems like a horrible use of such a meaningful term.

"I don't think they want anything to do with Enzo. His cousin has been trying to take over, and the entire family has been removing themselves from previous criminal enterprises. They won't come after you. And even if they did, I'll be with you. Always."

I don't want to start over. I love this town, my friends, and even my job. But I love my husband more. His dark green gaze is so intense. I have to tell him. "I'm not running again. The only reason I would leave is to stay with you."

He strokes his thumb down my tearstained cheek. "You want to stay with me, too?"

I nod, shyness stealing my words. But if I don't tell him what I want—exactly—how can my husband, my Dom, give me what I need? "Use your words" echoes through my head in

Tyler's dominant voice. There can be no ambiguity, no misunderstandings.

"I love you," I say. "I'm in love with you. I want our marriage, for better, for worse, with everything that being married entails. Rich, poor, good health and bad."

Tyler shifts his arm under my knees and lifts me onto his lap. His lips press to mine in sweet, soft kisses. "I love you, Amelia Kincaid Davis. I'm in for everything. Even kids." He freezes and locks his forest-green gaze on me. "If you're willing."

I snuggle into him, pressing my nose to his neck. He smells like cedar-tinged sweat, gunpowder, and safety. I relax against his chest.

"Think you might want kids someday?" he asks in a quiet, coaxing tone.

"I've never thought about it," I lie. The weight of all this trauma lifts a bit at his question. "I'm not against the idea. Especially the part where we make them." And the part where he's a dad, holding a baby in his arms. I see it so clearly, my breath catches.

He squeezes me tight and smacks my ass. "Naughty girl."

His growly tone of approval makes me squirm, and based on the hardening length beneath me, he's just as excited by the idea as I am. "Where would we live? The B and B isn't set up for kids. I can't imagine going up two flights of stairs with an infant or even pregnant. And I don't want to move back to St. Louis, even if it is safe now."

"How would you feel about a small relocation if we stay in the area, close to your friends?"

"What about the guys?" I glance up to find Stone on the phone. Who's he talking to this time, the airlines? "They're practically your family. You won't miss them?"

"They're staying here too. At least that's Stone's idea. He has to get Eliot and Cade on board."

"What? How?"

"Stone has an idea for a *private* resort he wants to build. All of us would be partners in the project."

"That sounds amazing." He's staying. The entire team is staying. A giddy rush vibrates through me. Everything I've dreamed of. After dancing with death, talking about life, and planning for our future, I need to be close to him. Reconnect on every level. Even if children never happen for us, my heart is bursting to full. We have a family. We are a family.

TWENTY-FIVE

Tyler

THE STORM PICKS UP AGAIN, the rain battering the huge windows like my heart pounds in my chest. I hold Amy tight, not willing to let one inch come between us. I haven't made a big deal about how close I came to losing her, but the attack could have ended up so differently. I press a kiss to her forehead, so damn grateful she's alive. She rests her head on my shoulder, slowly softening as the tension fades. We sit like that for a long time, neither of us anxious to break the connection.

Finally, Alex returns. The storm has blown itself out, and blue skies are peeking out amongst the lingering clouds. Stone offers to pitch in on the repairs.

They've got everything handled. "I'm taking Amy upstairs for a nap."

"Good call," Alex says.

Stone nods his approval, not that I need it, but it still alleviates my guilt at not offering to lend a hand.

"Let's go." I lift her off my lap. I'm sure she's in a strange place mentally, but I'll help her refocus, giving her exactly what she needs to let the trauma go. I'll always catch her. Always protect her. Always have her back.

With a click, I lock the bedroom door, glad for once to be so far away from the main floor. "Undress, love."

Amy spins, her eyes questioning. I don't move a muscle as I calmly hold her in my gaze. I can almost hear the moment her thinking clicks off.

She tugs up the bottom of her shirt.

I exhale for the first time since I issued the command. We'll be okay.

She removes her clothes, her eyes on me. Slipping her panties down her legs, she steps out and bends to pick up the pile.

"Wait."

She straightens. I slowly close the distance between us, place my hand on her shoulder, and drag my fingertips along her silky skin as I circle her, looking for any bruise or abrasion. I check each hand for burns. Nothing. Enzo didn't leave a mark, thankfully. At least none that I can see, but I'll still treat her with kid gloves. I pause behind her and remove my clothes. She must hear the sound of my zipper and see the pile of clothes added to hers. But she remains perfectly still. Such control. It only speaks to how much power she grants me when we're together like this. The tension in my shoulders and neck slips away. I embrace her, pressing my chest to her back, a silent thanks for all she is to me. I press soft kisses to her neck. Her warmth seeps deep inside me.

"Let's take a shower." I take her hand and lead her to the bathroom. I don't care how tiny the shower is. She needs this. I need this.

As the water heats, I run my hands up and down her arms,

over her breasts, along her belly that I imagine swelling with our child sometime in the future. I tease her curls, avoiding her clit. She juts her hips, demanding more with her body.

I retreat.

Her mewl of protest teases my cock.

She lets me care for every inch of her precious skin, murmuring words of approval. I shampoo her beautiful hair and rinse away all traces of the violence. I quickly soap myself, washing off the hospital, the fear, the garbage scent of that foul monster I was far too close to. After I turn off the water, I carefully dry Amy's skin and squeeze the water from her darkened hair. I love the nearly silent cocoon we've created as I care for her, but I'm about to break it. She needs more.

"Wait for me on the bed," I say. As she leaves the bathroom, I'm unable to resist and tap her creamy globe.

She squeaks with a tiny hop.

I hold back my grin. She's fucking adorable. That squeak will be a cry of pleasure shortly. I take my time, drying off completely, giving my cock a few tugs, promising more soon. I hang up the towels and stop in the doorway.

Fuck.

Amy is on the bed but not sprawled out as I expected. Instead, her knees are on the edge of the bed, ass in the air, pussy wet and shiny with her arousal. She's dropped to her elbows, her head resting between them.

She clearly knows what she wants. And I'm the luckiest man on the planet because she wants me. Her beautiful wet pussy can't be ignored. I press two fingers into her heat, stretching and sliding. I savor her gasp. She's so hot. So fucking tight. "Are you my good girl?"

"Yes, Tyler. Always. Forever."

Her words hit me hard. My balls twitch, and my cock dances with the desire to reward her. I slide my fingers in and out of her sweet cunt. Faster. Her slick cream coats me. I pull away and dip my thumb in, only to quickly return my fingers to her channel while I use her slick juices to rub her puckered hole.

"Please," she whimpers.

"I love the way you beg." I free my hand and smack her ass with my other. She inspires me to push her hips forward, placing her in the perfect position to bury my face in her pussy and feast. She tastes so fucking good. I can't lap up her juices fast enough. She quivers, nearly a thrust. I spank her again.

"Yes." She wiggles her ass and looks back at me with a smile.

I have to bite back my grin. "Hold still."

It's a bullshit demand. There's no way she'll be able to remain unmoving with what I'm doing. I dive back in, savoring the salty, sweet flavor that is uniquely hers. The taste I won't let be far from my lips for the rest of my life. So fucking perfect. She deserves all the pleasure I can give her. I add my fingers to the effort, fucking her while I eat her out. Based on the fluttering squeezes, she's on the edge. I lick her ass, bury my fingers deep, and thumb her clit.

She screams my name, her hips jutting back, her pussy clamping down on my hand. I work her through every last tremor before she collapses. Pride rolls through me. But we aren't done yet.

Her silky skin is irresistible. I stroke her from her shoulder to her lower back, stopping before I get to her sculpted ass. Time for the next phase of my plan to wipe the day from her mind. "Stand up for me."

She turns her head and side-eyes me.

Yeah, I'm not going to feel bad about this at all. "Now."

She startles at my tone and shifts to her feet. I grip her elbow since she's still a bit wobbly. After I sit on the edge of the bed, still warm from her body heat, I pat my lap. "I want to spank you."

"Okay." The heat in her gaze confirms my plan.

"Over my knee."

She carefully places her naked form on my bare legs, and I'm in heaven. I rub circles along the sweet flesh I'm about to turn red, mostly to get myself under control. My cock is quite happy to be pinned between her side and my abdomen. Only one place would be better, but that comes later.

"Do you want me to spank you?"

"God, yes." Her breathy voice is desperate.

"Tyler."

"Yes, Tyler." Her small chuckle dispels the last of my lingering tension. "*Please.*"

The please nearly does me in. I take a light touch initially, bringing the blood to her muscles and warming her up. Then I add force to the impact as I go. My hand will give out before her ass. Hopefully, she gives out before my hand. The steady rhythm I maintain should be hypnotic. The pain will morph into pleasure. "Spread your legs."

She shifts, opening herself to me.

I clutch her tighter. Spank her lower, a teasing threat.

Her panting breaths call to me to do more. A little harder. A little faster. There. She softens, relaxing completely into my hold. Tears stream down my thigh as she silently cries. I land two bold blows at the tops of her thighs, and she squeals, arching her back. I plunge my hand between her legs and pinch her swollen clit, sending her flying. I rub each tender globe, loving the way her cum spills across my thigh. She's boneless on my lap when she finally settles down from her high, but I'm aching for more.

I guide her to the mattress.

"I want you, Amy." I'm desperate to make love to my

perfect wife. The woman I've nearly lost so many times. I cling to her, waiting for her answer.

She nods.

"Words, baby." I tuck a strand of hair behind her ear and dab a stray tear from her cheek.

"Make love to me, Tyler. I need you inside me." Her sweet brown eyes pull me in deep. "Wipe away everything but you."

Tears prick my eyes. That's exactly what I need, to erase everything but her—but us. I shift between her long legs, positioning myself at her entrance and returning home. Her wet heat welcomes me. She wraps her legs around me, clutching me close. She glides her hands over my cheeks and into my hair. I fall deep into her eyes before I shift my arms under her shoulders and pull her into a kiss. Slowly, I pulse in and out, prolonging this perfect moment. Every part of us connected. Her breath is my breath. Her heart beats with mine. Our bodies, our lives, no longer separate.

Every day. I will find a way to make sure this, right here, happens every day forever. I couldn't handle living without her ever again.

TWENTY-SIX

Amy

I'VE BEEN in a state of bliss since Tyler took me upstairs yesterday. He's barely let me out of his sight, much less our bed. The sun isn't even up when I sneak out of our room. His attention was exactly what I needed to get over the shock of the attack, but now it's time I reclaim my space. My B and B. My kitchen.

I pause when I cross the threshold. My kettle is back in place, no trace of the water on the floor. But I can see what happened clearly. A shiver grips me, but I shake it off and turn on the oven. Moving to the kettle, I refill it and start it heating. I toss the hand towels I'd had hanging down the stairs to the basement and pick out a fresh set, placing them just so next to the sink and over the handle of the oven.

I lightly stir the scone mix until the batter is just moistened. As soon as the tray is in the oven, I pour a fresh cup of tea. A special blend of lemon and mint, perfect for watching the sunrise while the scones bake. I clutch the warm mug and stare out the dining room windows. Soft pink light peaks over the pine-covered ridge. The chill in the morning air has seeped into the house. The first snow could hit any day now.

This is what I dreamed of my entire life—a home in a beautiful setting filled with people who matter to me. People I love. If what Tyler said is true, he wants this life too. I have no reason to doubt him. But are they all really preparing to move to Colorado permanently?

Stone comes down the stairs, freshly shaved and showered. "Morning."

"Good morning, Stone. Coffee? I can start it now, and the scones should be done in just a—" The chime of the timer interrupts me. "Well, now."

"Coffee'd be great."

I duck into the kitchen. The man still kind of scares the crap out of me. I know what he did when he took me for the drive, playing devil's advocate and making me think about my commitment to Tyler. All the while, he was making plans to keep everyone here. I can't be angry at him. He's ten steps ahead of everyone all the time.

Stone takes his full mug from the machine while I move the scones to a cooling rack. Tyler and Alex appear a moment later. Alex beelines for the coffee while Tyler saunters over to me.

"Missed you, Mrs. Davis," he murmurs in my ear, wrapping me in a tight squeeze. My insides flutter at his tone, hinting at my misbehavior. It's a tease but effective. I receive his kiss, but before we can get too far out of hand with a public display, Stone's phone rings.

"Eliot." He puts the call on speaker.

I brace for bad news but pray it's good.

"Just wanted to let everyone know Blake made it through the night. He's breathing on his own, and there's been no swelling around his brain. Thank God for airbags." Eliot sounds exhausted but hopeful.

"That's good. That's really good," Stone replies with a hitch in his voice.

It's such a small step but so promising. I take a shuddering breath of relief. Tyler wraps me in a brief hug. Even Alex nods with a slight smile.

"Yeah, he's fighting. Cade's in with him now. We aren't leaving him alone at all. Doc's approved it since his vitals improve when one of us is with him. He's staying in the ICU for at least today, maybe tomorrow. Then we go to critical care."

"Do you need anything?" Tyler asks, his face pinched with concern and maybe a bit of guilt. I thread my fingers through his.

"We're good," Eliot replies. "Pierce has been taking excellent care of us. Meal breaks, transportation. And I don't know how you found that house so close to the hospital, but it's perfect. I'm not sure how we're going to repay—"

"Don't worry about anything except taking care of our boy." Stone crosses his arms as if Eliot can see him adopt his Dom pose. Although I'm sure his tone carries even through the speakerphone. "Everything will be ready and waiting when he gets discharged."

"Call if you need *anything*, man," Alex says from his position against the counter. His casual pose contradicts the concern in his voice.

As soon as they end the call, I start moving the scones to a plate, taking them and the butter to the table. Tyler follows with dishes and silverware.

"I can make eggs," I say.

"This is fine. If we need eggs, we can make them." Tyler kisses me and pulls me onto a chair. I'm not used to sitting with my guests. But they aren't my guests. They're my family. "You guys will stay here at the Sunflower, right?"

"Don't you need to rent these rooms? And winter is high season, right?" Alex asks.

"I want you here." I can economize, and I have some savings. It's worth it to take care of them the way they've taken care of me.

"Could be a while before the project is far enough along to move in." Stone's gaze is like a physical thing, touching me.

"I still have three rooms I can rent, at least until Blake is ready to come home."

Alex sets his knife, loaded with butter, on his plate and stares at me. A smile teases at Stone's lips, which is either endearing or terrifying. I can't decide which. Tyler tugs me to him and kisses my head.

"What?" I ask.

"Do you mean it? Is this our home?" Alex questions me.

"Of course I mean it. Wherever Tyler is, that's my home. You're his family. Our family. So this is home for as long as we need it."

The smile on Stone's face is warm and not terrifying at all. He gives me a curt nod and picks up his phone, placing whoever he's dialed on speaker.

"Thank you," Tyler whispers over the ringing.

I should be thanking him, but it doesn't matter. Families don't keep score. And besides, they saved my life, so the score would always be in their favor anyway.

"Hey, Stone." The man he called sounds friendly. "What's up?"

"Where are we with the property?"

"I put in your offer as soon as you told me. The seller is out of town, but they have to respond by five tonight. I'll call as soon as I hear anything."

Stone finishes his call and locks his gaze on me. "What else do you need done here to be ready to rent rooms?"

"Nothing. Everything has been painted. The new linens are ready to go. I just have to remove the block on the rooms." I lick the last of the lemon scone crumbs from my fingers.

"Make sure. Because once we close on that building, it will be all hands on deck. Even yours, G-man."

"Former G-man. Now I'm just Amy's man." Tyler stands up. "And as soon as she finishes with whatever needs to happen to open up the reservations, I'm taking her back to bed." He tugs me up from the chair. "I missed my morning sex." He slaps my ass, the sting going right through my jeans, and I jump.

Alex's and Stone's laughter, along with Tyler's, follows me into my office and I love it.

"Hurry, I need you back in bed." Tyler isn't quite pulling off the dominant tone he's capable of.

I roll my eyes at my husband.

"Oh, naughty girl. You'll regret that."

I won't. Not. At. All.

EPILOGUE

Tyler

I FOLD the newspaper and leave it face up on the dining table where everyone in the house can see the headline: *Killer Gets Life*. It's been months, but the authorities moved incredibly fast to finalize Enzo Junior's conviction. I have a feeling his "family" assisted with expediting the process. I'm just glad Amy didn't have to testify. I pick up my dishes and take them to the kitchen.

Has she seen the paper? We have a guest coming today. I can't let her be rattled over the reminder of what happened last fall. She's in her tiny office, head down, muttering about whatever she's working on. Her fingers fly over the numeric keypad. This will be fun. I move to her side, then place one hand on her chairback and the other on the desk. "Mrs. Davis. What do you think you're doing?"

She lifts her gaze to mine. Her wide doe eyes are exactly the reaction I shot for with my pissed-off agent voice.

"Under the terms of your protection agreement, are you allowed to do anything with numbers?" I lean closer.

"What are you talking about?" Her forehead wrinkles, and I have to hold back a grin. She hasn't figured out my game yet.

"Are you or are you not doing accounting work?" I fight to keep the teasing out of my tone as she goes from startled to angry.

"I'm doing the taxes for the partnership. They're due in a week." The scowl on her face is priceless.

I turn her chair and place my hands on the armrests, giving her my best hardass glower. "Under the terms of your protection agreement, you're being a very *naughty* girl."

She shivers. The creases in her forehead relax. "Am I, *Agent* Davis?"

"As your handler, it's my job to remind you of what you're allowed to do." I match her sultry tone. "You can't do any accounting."

She squirms in her chair, and my dick twitches. "I'll do accounting if I want to."

I lift her to stand. "I'm here to protect you. Make sure you *obey* the rules."

Her hands go to her hips. "What are you going to do about it, *Agent* Davis?"

I grin. There's my sassy sub. I bend at the knees and throw her over my shoulder. She squeals, gripping my waistband. I smack her ass as we leave the office. Alex nods to me as we pass by the dining table on the way to the stairs. I meet Stone on the landing.

"Help," Amy cries to him.

Stone snorts. I pause and present her ass. He gives her a light smack. "Looks like Tyler has everything well in hand."

"Hey," Amy calls to him as he descends the stairway we just came up.

"Help is not your safe word, Amy," Stone calls back.

Amy laughs. "Traitor."

"What?" Stone pauses on the last stair, and I turn to meet his gaze. I give her ass several hard smacks. He nods and disappears.

She kicks her feet ineffectively. "No fair."

I pepper her ass all the way to the attic bedroom. "You break the rules, you face the consequences."

"Promise?"

"Always." I slide her down my front and kiss her, letting all my pent-up concern for her well-being release. Until the trial was final, anything could have gone wrong. But it didn't. She's safe. She's here. She's mine. And I'm hers. "But first, I believe we have some bad behavior we need to address."

"I have been bad. Very bad." She wriggles out of her sweater and unclasps her bra.

She's stunning. Every time I see her, she takes my breath away. I caress her, cupping a breast in each hand, pinching her nipples, teasing her. She arches into my hold, and I slap her tit, leaving a very faint handprint. The audible catch of her breath excites me. There's a fire in her gaze. Her moan practically a purr. Relief floods me. I've only ever spanked her bottom, but I want to explore everything with her. I slap the other tit for balance. "Take off your pants."

She scrambles to obey. The risk I took was rewarded based on how fast she was willing to get naked for me. I tug my sweater over my head and undo the button on my jeans to give my cock some breathing room. I'm aching to slide into her wet heat, but I started this scene and plan to finish it. Take her to the space where she's completely relaxed, floating in her trust for me, knowing I will never let her down.

I widen my stance. "Kneel."

She lowers herself, her mouth slightly agape. My strong,

independent, confident wife assumes the picture of a willing sub. She undoes me, and I will do the same for her.

I shove my jeans down my hips and shift closer, teasing her beautiful mouth with the tip of my cock. She relaxes her jaw, inviting me in. Her gaze locks on mine. I squeeze my shaft to control my response as a drop of precum beads at the tip. Unable to resist, I paint her lip with the moisture. The pink of her tongue poking out to lap up my taste is like a stroke to my balls. "Open."

The corners of her mouth tilt up before she opens wide, allowing me inside. Her warm brown eyes sparkle with love. I tease her, dancing my tip in and out, exactly the way we both like. She leans forward to chase me. That's the sign. I grip her hair and slide all the way in. Her tongue wiggles on my shaft. I'm not going to last.

She holds me in her mouth as I thrust in and out. The energy at the base of my spine builds. Her sweet caresses, her loving gaze, the way she hollows her cheeks each time I slide out fills me with pride, with belonging, with complete trust in her and our future.

Not yet. I stop. Free myself from her perfect caress. I stroke her hair. "My sweet love. You take me so well."

I step back and tug my jeans up. Time to retake control. Not that I gave it away, but she owned me with that blow job, and I need to return the favor. But first, we have a scene to finish. "I believe you have a spanking due."

Leaving her on her knees, I sit on the edge of the bed. "Come here."

She crawls to me. And all at once, my balls swell like I'm the king of the world. I did not fucking expect that. Damn. My cock twitches, threatening to explode in my jeans. Not yet. I pat my denim-covered lap. "Right here, my naughty girl."

She has a spark in her eyes as she eagerly arranges herself

on my lap, legs parted. There will never be better moments in my life than when my naked wife is willing to give me control, splayed over my thighs, ass high in the air, waiting for my attention. I place one hand on her lower back to hold her in place and trail the fingers of my other hand up her inner thigh. Heat radiates off her pussy. I slide my fingers into her hot, wet opening. "Did you like sucking my cock?"

"Yes, Sir."

I already had my answer, but I love hearing her breathless agreement. I fuck her with two fingers in a slow, teasing pace. Her back tenses. She's fighting to remain still, but I won't let her. I thrust faster, teasing her clit with my thumb. Her hips lift, and I stop.

"No," she wails, demanding the orgasm she almost had.

I spank her ass. I can't keep my hands off her, and I don't want to. "What?"

"Please, Sir. Let me come." She kicks her feet.

I laugh. "No." This is the fun part, the part we both love. I spank her faster, harder until I've covered every inch of her flesh. The red-hot heat is exactly what we craved. Unable to resist, I rub the heat deep into her flesh. As soon as she relaxes, I hold her in place, slap her sopping pussy, and then slide two digits in deep. She moans my name. My chest swells. She so wet—for me. She makes me feel like a hero. Her hero. I bring her juices to her clit and tease and pinch until she's screaming her release. "That's one."

She's limp on my lap. I rub her back in slow circles until she comes back to her body. I want to give her so many orgasms that she forgets any bad thing that ever happened. "Up on the bed." She's wobbly, so I keep my arm around her.

"Yes, Sir."

"Hands and knees." She follows the instructions, but I hesitate. That juicy pussy is calling my name, but should I eat her or fuck her.

"Please fuck me, Tyler. Please."

Any other day, I'd eat her out first for no other reason than to deny her request. But there is no way I can delay anchoring my body to hers when she honors me with such sweet submission. I yank off my jeans and crawl up behind her. With one single move, I thrust into her hot heat until my balls slap against her clit.

"More," she demands.

I grab her hips and rut into her hard and fast. The way she squeezes me and her cries of pleasure stroke my ego. My balls are filling again already.

"Rub your clit. I want you to come as hard and as fast as you can."

She rushes to obey, and within moments, her wet, fluttering contractions build in power enough to drag me into space with her. We soar on waves of ecstasy, leaving everything behind, moored only to each other. Slowly, we float back down. I collapse, still lodged inside, and roll us to our sides. Yeah, I could die a happy man spooned around the love of my life, cock embedded deep inside her.

I smooth the hair back from her face. "You okay?"

She wiggles her butt against me. "Perfect."

We rest in silence, our breath synchronizing to a normal rhythm. Unable to avoid the topic any longer, I ask the question looming around us. "Did you see the paper?"

"I did." Her tone is neutral.

"How do you feel about it?"

She's slow to answer. "Relieved but angry. Going to prison forever doesn't change the fact he killed people and took away Blake's future."

I squeeze her tighter. "We're making sure Blake has a future waiting for him when he's released from rehab."

Blake was transferred from the hospital to a rehab center. His legs have healed, but he's still not walking. I have no idea if he ever will again. Neither does he, and he's pissed about it. I don't blame him.

A heaviness settles around us. I need to change the mood. "Did I show you the logo Stone commissioned?"

"No." She cranes her neck to face me. "Do you have it?"

I regretfully leave her body to retrieve my phone from my discarded jeans and pull up the text with the image. She grabs my hand and turns the phone toward her.

"Really?' She chuckles. "The Yacht Club?"

"It's perfect when you think about it. It's an ideal cover, and if you look carefully, the oars on the logo are actually paddles. Alex was really pleased with the rope. We're targeting the wealthy, the vacationers, the people Pandora doesn't serve."

"But there's no ocean for miles."

"There's a lake. People have sailboats here. Besides, I like the irony."

"I do too." She pulls the screen to her, inspecting the life preserver logo with the hidden BDSM elements. Kind of like the dungeon will be—if you know, you know.

"We'll have to help test some of the equipment before we can open it to members." I say this as if it's some kind of burden.

"Quality checks are important." She smiles at me, clearly on the same train of thought.

"Might have to test the spanking bench a couple of times—"

"Just to be sure."

I leave my phone on the nightstand to pull her into my arms and kiss her deeply. Having her safe, committed to me, and a part of my family leaves me with confidence and contentment that we can handle anything the future brings as long as we're together.

———————

Alex

I grab my tools from the bed of Gabe's truck and give him a wave, letting him know he can head home. I like working with Amy's friend. He knows construction, knows how to lead a crew, and he ain't a slacker. Even had his brother come out to help on the project during some of the earlier trickier parts. After a long day of framing, I'm due for a shower.

There's a little red car in the front drive. Shiny except for the road dust on the lower panels. Rental. That means our guest has arrived. I wipe my feet on the mat before I go inside the Sunflower.

Standing at the high table Amy uses to hold her guest book, its drawer filled with keys, is a woman who is straight out of my spank bank. Mile-long legs wrapped in jeans and boots with a perfect peach of an ass. Auburn hair down to the middle of her lean back. I swallow the urge to whistle and slap my cap on my thigh before I wrangle her into my bed. Whoa. Nope. I take a step back.

"Hey, Alex." Amy calls out to me before I can disappear up the stairs.

"Amy. Ma'am." I nod at the fantasy woman. My mama raised me right. "How're y'all doin'?"

"This is Sonja Redding. She's staying with us for a few weeks."

Weeks?

The woman turns and punches me in the chest with her blue eyes, freckled nose, and full lips. She smiles. "Hi, Alex."

Aw, hell no. Danger flashes all around this woman. I should run while I can.

"Since you're going up, could you show her to the Columbine room?" I know exactly which room she means, but she doesn't understand what she's asking. I should be staying as far away from this woman as possible, not escorting her to her bedroom.

"Yes, ma'am," I say, despite my red flags. "That your bag?" I point at the carry-on roller.

"I can get it." Sonja's voice is like a soft breeze on a hot summer day. Damn. It's like someone custom-designed a woman just for me.

"No, ma'am." I pick it up by the side handle and proceed up the stairs, tools in one hand, bag in the other, dick leading the way to her room. No. No. No.

"You work construction?" she asks.

"Yes, ma'am." And because my mama raised me right, I ask, "And you?"

"I'm a writer. My agent booked this place for me so I can finish a novel. I should have had it done months ago. He says it's to remove distractions."

I've never met a writer. I glance back. She's staring at my ass. It appears we're both distracted. I can't let that happen. Ever. I stop at her room and set her bag down. She unlocks the door, letting it swing open wide. The slightly purple-blue paint Amy had us put on the walls last fall contrasts perfectly with Sonja's hair. "Anything else?"

A light blush hits her cheeks. Sweet baby Jesus, help me.

"I, uh, have a bigger bag in the car..." She blinks up at me with those baby blues.

"Sure." I hold out my hand. "Keys?"

She digs in the pocket of her jeans, drawing my eyes to the apex of her legs. Nope. I drag my gaze to her face like I didn't just see an image of us fucking with her in a rope swing.

She drops the keys on my palm.

I spin. "Be back."

I leave my tools inside my room only to find Sonja still watching me from her doorway. She knows where my room is.

Dang it.

I trot down the stairs and pop the trunk on her car. A huge bag with airline tags still attached fills the space. I heft it out. She has to have small children packed in there as much as it weighs. I set the bag on the ground and lock her car. Curiosity wins. I lift the printed tag. DFW.

Fuck. My. Life. She's from Texas.

I heave the bag back to her room and knock on the door. She opens it so fast she must have been waiting.

"Here you go."

She steps back, inviting me in. My heart pounds a warning tattoo against my ribs. My dick hollers, "Yee haw!" My dick is dumb. I push the bag over the threshold. "Have a nice stay."

Before she can say anything else, I pivot and practically run back to my room. For the first time since I came to the Sunflower, I lock my door.

In the shower, I take care of all the dirt and sweat, and jack myself off to my favorite imaginary woman who suddenly looks a lot like Sonja. Not good.

I towel off and toss on my sweats commando. I type her name into the browser on my phone. Nothing. No author by that name.

It don't mean nothing. I'm just being paranoid. Lots of authors don't publish under their real names. Besides, it's not like I'll be hanging around here. I'll be busy with the construction of the club. The downstairs is basically done, and we've finished framing out the restaurant. The first two condos just need paint and fixtures. They're fully accessible to ADA standards. We're just waiting for the inspection. Should be perfect timing for Blake getting out of rehab.

I can keep my head down and my hands to myself until the club opens. Once it does, I can express myself in a safe place—with plenty of witnesses. And no Sonja.

ACKNOWLEDGMENTS

First, last, and always, thank you to my husband for supporting my writing in every way. I love you!

Thank you to the Red Reines for everything you do.

Thank you to Brandi Doane McCann for another amazing cover and the fabulous series logo.

Thank you to Jenny Sims for the fantastic editing. Readers, please know that any errors you find while reading this book are mine, not hers. I'm incorrigible.

Thank you to my amazing beta readers who made this book infinitely better.

Thank you to Passionate Ink for providing a safe and educational forum for erotic authors.

And, most importantly, thank you to my readers who make it worth all the struggles to write!

ABOUT THE AUTHOR

Award-winning, best-selling author, Jordyn Kross, is an unapologetically naughty novelist who spent years honing her writing skills with tech manuals and marginal poetry before finding her passion for writing sexy, boundary-stretching happily-ever-afters.

When she's not writing, she's attempting to garden in the desert Southwest, hiking with her insane pound posse, and admiring that handsome man wandering around her house who continues to stay.

Jordyn enjoys saucy double entendres, pretending to be an extrovert, and is well-known for having no filter. And when she's not in social media jail, she can be found on Facebook, Instagram, and BookBub, or hiding in a dark cave peering out at the X file formerly knows as Twitter.